"He's opening the portal!"

Directly behind where Professor Vance was standing, Jake saw the temporal portal materialize—first as a small pulsating dot that hung in midair, then rapidly expanding until it became a human-sized rectangle.

The portal flickered for a moment, but the Changeling Vance adjusted the remote device, and the portal stabilized. "Now I have the only key that unlocks the door to the past."

With that, he turned and stepped into the portal.

And then he was gone.

"Where's he going?" Jake asked.

"Wherever it is, we've got to stop him!" Nog yelled, running toward the portal.

"Nog! Wait!" Jake shouted. But it was too late. The Ferengi had already entered the vortex.

Jake hesitated only a moment. The portal was shrinking. It would close in another moment—with Nog and the Changeling trapped on the other side. Jake had no idea where he was about to go, but he knew he couldn't desert his best friend. He ran into the vortex—and vanished.

Star Trek: The Next Generation
STARFLEET ACADEMY

#1 Worf's First Adventure
#2 Line of Fire
#3 Survival
#4 Capture the Flag
#5 Atlantis Station
#6 Mystery of the Missing Crew
#7 The Secret of the Lizard People
#8 Starfall
#9 Nova Command
#10 Loyalties
#11 Crossfire
#12 Breakaway
#13 The Haunted Starship

StarTrek:
STARFLEET ACADEMY

#1 Crisis on Vulcan
#2 Aftershock
#3 Cadet Kirk

Star Trek: Deep Space Nine

#1 The Star Ghost
#2 Stowaways
#3 Prisoners of Peace
#4 The Pet
#5 Arcade
#6 Field Trip
#7 Gypsy World
#8 Highest Score
#9 Cardassian Imps
#10 Space Camp
#11 Day of Honor: Honor Bound
#12 Trapped in Time

Star Trek: Voyager
STARFLEET ACADEMY

#1 Lifeline
#2 The Chance Factor
#3 Quarantine

Star Trek movie tie-ins

Star Trek Generations
Star Trek First Contact

Available from Minstrel Books

For orders other than by individual consumers, Pocket Books grants a discount on the purchase of **10 or more** copies of single titles for special markets or premium use. For further details, please write to the Vice-President of Special Markets, Pocket Books, 1633 Broadway, New York, NY 10019-6785, 8th Floor.

For information on how individual consumers can place orders, please write to Mail Order Department, Simon & Schuster Inc., 200 Old Tappan Road, Old Tappan, NJ 07675.

TRAPPED IN TIME

TED PEDERSEN

**Interior illustrations by
Todd Cameron Hamilton**

Published by POCKET BOOKS
New York   London   Toronto   Sydney   Tokyo   Singapore

The sale of this book without its cover is unauthorized. If you purchased this book without a cover, you should be aware that it was reported to the publisher as "unsold and destroyed." Neither the author nor the publisher has received payment for the sale of this "stripped book."

This book is a work of fiction. Names, characters, places and incidents are products of the author's imagination or are used fictitiously. Any resemblance to actual events or locales or persons living or dead is entirely coincidental.

A MINSTREL PAPERBACK *Original*

A Minstrel Book published by
POCKET BOOKS, a division of Simon & Schuster Inc.
1230 Avenue of the Americas, New York, NY 10020

Copyright © 1998 by Paramount Pictures. All rights reserved.

STAR TREK is a Registered Trademark of Paramount Pictures.

A VIACOM COMPANY

This book is published by Pocket Books, a division of Simon & Schuster Inc., under exclusive license from Paramount Pictures.

All rights reserved, including the right to reproduce this book or portions thereof in any form whatsoever. For information address Pocket Books, 1230 Avenue of the Americas, New York, NY 10020

ISBN: 0-671-01440-4

First Minstrel Books printing February 1998

10 9 8 7 6 5 4 3 2 1

A MINSTREL BOOK and colophon are registered trademarks of Simon & Schuster Inc.

Cover art by Alan Gutierrez
Interior illustrations by Todd Cameron Hamilton

Printed in the U.S.A.

To Brandy and all her friends

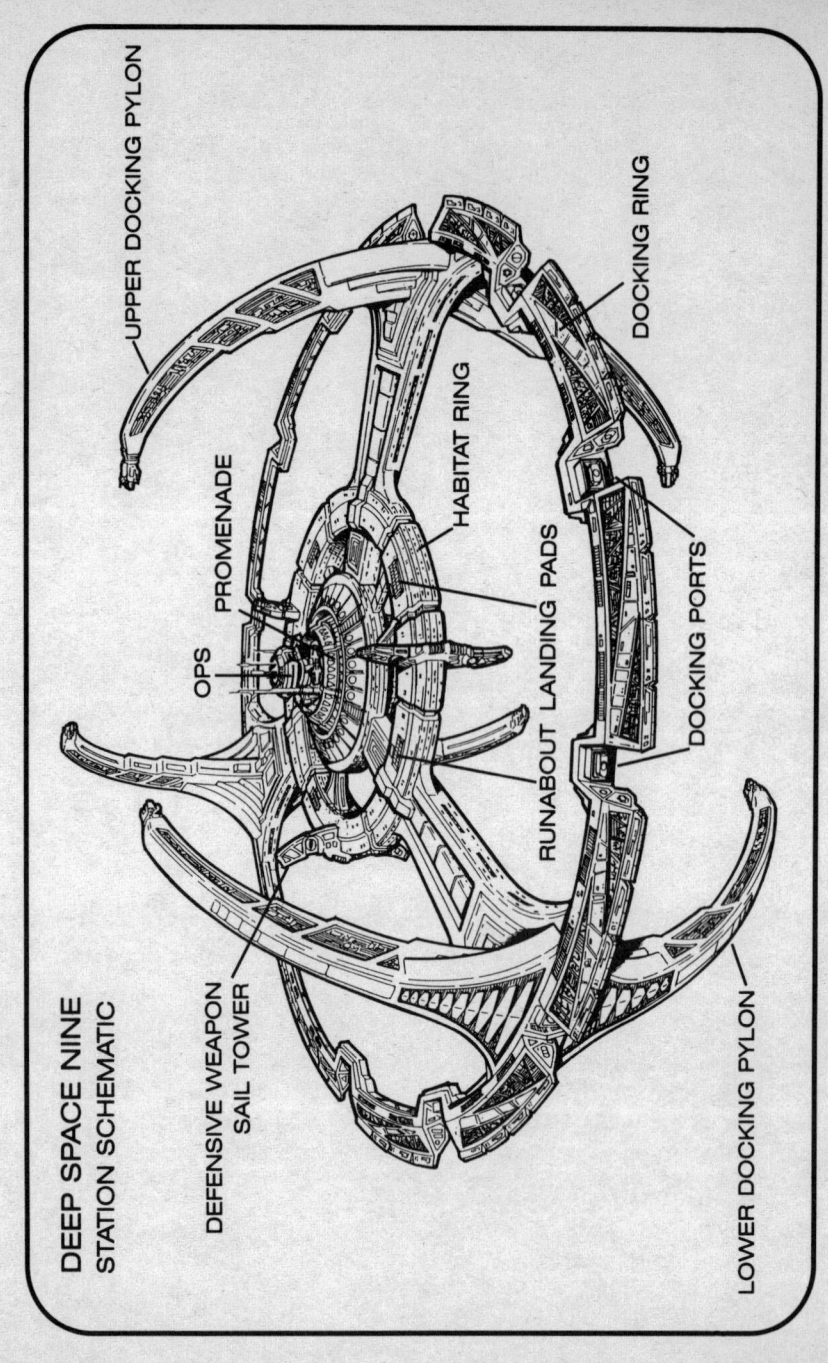

STAR TREK: DEEP SPACE NINE®
Cast of Characters

JAKE SISKO—Jake is a young teenager and the only human boy permanently on board *Deep Space Nine*. Jake's mother died when he was very young. He came to the space station with his father but found very few kids his own age. He doesn't remember life on Earth, but he loves baseball and candy bars, and he hates homework. His father doesn't approve of his friendship with Nog.

NOG—He is a Ferengi boy whose primary goal in life—like all Ferengi—is to make money. His father, Rom, is frequently away on business, which is fine with Nog. His uncle, Quark, keeps an eye on him. Nog thinks humans are odd with their notions of trust and favors and friendship. He doesn't always understand Jake, but since his father forbids him to hang out with the human boy, Nog and Jake are best friends. Nog loves to play tricks on people, but he tries to avoid Odo whenever possible.

COMMANDER BENJAMIN SISKO—Jake's father has been appointed by Starfleet Command to oversee the operations of the space station and act as a liaison between the Federation and Bajor. His wife was killed in a Borg attack, and he is raising Jake by himself. He is a very busy man who always tries to make time for his son.

ODO—The security officer was found by Bajoran scientists years ago, but Odo has no idea where he originally came from. He is a shape shifter, and thus can assume any shape for a period of time. He normally maintains a vaguely human appearance but every sixteen hours he must revert to his natural liquid state. He has no patience for lawbreakers and less for Ferengi.

MAJOR KIRA NERYS—Kira was a freedom fighter in the Bajoran underground during the Cardassian occupation of Bajor. She now represents Bajoran interests aboard the station and is Sisko's first officer. Her temper is legendary.

LIEUTENANT JADZIA DAX—An old friend of Commander Sisko's, the science officer Dax is actually two joined entities known as the Trill. There is a separate consciousness—a symbiont—in the young female host's body. Sisko knew the symbiont Dax in a previous host, which was a "he."

DR. JULIAN BASHIR—Eager for adventure, Doctor Bashir graduated at the top of his class and requested a deep-space posting. His enthusiasm sometimes gets him into trouble.

MILES O'BRIEN—Formerly the Transporter Chief aboard the *U.S.S. Enterprise,* O'Brien is now Chief of Operations on Deep Space Nine.

KEIKO O'BRIEN—Keiko was a botanist on the *Enterprise,* but she moved to the station with her husband and her young daughter, Molly. Since there is little use for her botany skills on the station, she is the teacher for all of the permanent and traveling students.

QUARK—Nog's uncle and a Ferengi businessman by trade, Quark runs his own combination restaurant/casino/holosuite venue on the Promenade, the central meeting place for much of the activity on the station. Quark has his hand in every deal on board and usually manages to stay just one step ahead of the law—usually in the shape of Odo.

Historian's note: The events of this series take place during the first and second seasons of the *Deep Space Nine* television show.

TRAPPED IN TIME

PROLOGUE

Deep Space Nine, Alpha Quadrant

Just talking to them makes me feel guilty," Jake Sisko said while waiting anxiously in the commander's office on the Ops deck of *Deep Space Nine*.

"Don't worry about it, Jake. They're only here because a report has to be filed. Nog will be going through the same process back at Starfleet Academy." This calm reassurance from his father, Captain Benjamin Sisko, commander of the Bajoran space station, did little to quiet the butterflies in Jake's stomach.

Jake knew there was nothing to worry about, but the prospect of being interrogated by the Department of Temporal Investigations was still emotionally unsettling. He should be feeling like a hero, but instead he was acting like a kid about to face the principal for disciplining.

"Relax," the elder Sisko said. "This will all be over in less than an hour."

At that moment, Sisko's commbadge chirped. "Yes?" he said in response.

"They're here," answered the voice of Major Kira Nerys, the Bajoran liaison to the station and Sisko's second-in-command.

"Send them in."

Jake watched the door to the office slide open and two of the most straightlaced, expressionless Starfleet officers he had ever seen enter. They looked as if they had been cloned from the same mold.

"I am Dulmur," the slightly taller one on the right said. "This is Lusly," he added, indicating his partner. They both took seats without waiting to be invited and opened their identical thin black briefcases.

"Welcome to *Deep Space Nine,*" Sisko said. "If there is anything—"

"We would like to talk to the subject in private," Dulmur interrupted.

"I'd like my father to stay," Jake said.

"If that's all right," Sisko quickly added.

The two temporal policemen exchanged expressionless glances. "No. It's not all right," Lusly said.

"Standard operating procedures. No one not personally involved in the temporal displacement is allowed to be present during debriefing."

"But I am his father, as well as commander of this station," Sisko argued.

TRAPPED IN TIME

"I'm afraid in this situation we outrank you," Dulmur said flatly.

Sisko was about to argue, then looked over at Jake, thought better of it, and smiled. "I'll be in Ops if you need me." He patted his son's shoulder and left.

When the door had closed behind Sisko, the two temporal policemen turned their full attention to Jake. "In your own words, tell us exactly what happened."

"It will take some time," Jake said.

Lusly looked at Dulmur. "Why do they always say that?"

"Perhaps an attempt at humor," Dulmur said. Then he looked at Jake and almost smiled. "We have all the time in the world. Please begin."

Jake began to tell his story, "It started on Earth, right after the Changeling threat and the near takeover of the Federation by a radical group of Starfleet officers."

"We're well aware of the failed coup by Admiral Leyton," Dulmur said.

"What we want to know about are the events that happened afterward," Lusly added.

"I'm getting to that," Jake said. "If you'll let me."

"Sorry," Dulmur said. "Please continue."

"I guess the best place to start is in New Orleans, at Grandpa Joe's restaurant. It was the weekend, and I was having lunch with Nog...."

CHAPTER 1

Earth, New Orleans, Three Weeks Earlier

"Your grandfather serves the best tube grubs on Earth," Nog said, munching down the wriggling morsels with obvious relish.

"He serves the *only* tube grubs on Earth," Jake replied, doing his best to look away while his Ferengi friend crunched on his lunch. Nog might be his best friend, but Jake was still uncomfortable with Ferengi eating habits. "Careful not to get any of those on your uniform."

Nog wore a freshly replicated Starfleet Academy cadet uniform and was being extremely careful to keep it that way. It was apparent that being in Starfleet, even though he was only halfway through his first semester, had made quite an impact on Nog. He seemed a lot more grown-up.

But then, Jake thought, they were both older and

wiser since those early days on *Deep Space Nine* when Nog was always getting into trouble and Jake was the straightlaced son of the station's commander.

Fraternizing with a Ferengi was something Jake's father had firmly opposed. Nog's father held the same low opinion about Nog's association with the human boy Jake. But being the only kids of their age on the station, it was only natural that they would start to pal around together.

In the beginning they hung together as a form of rebellion against their fathers, but it didn't take long for them to become real friends. Over the years their friendship had grown, and now both fathers reluctantly admitted that the two boys had been good for each other.

Which was why Jake had been both sad and happy when Nog sold off his childhood possessions—as Ferengi do to raise capital when they are about to embark on their life's career—and left the space station to attend Starfleet Academy on Earth.

Deep Space Nine was an isolated island in the Bajoran star system, and without someone Jake could share his experiences with, it shrank even more.

While Nog hit the books, or whatever it was that first-year cadets did at the Academy, Jake found himself spending less time in the Promenade and more time hunched over his PADD. The adventures the two boys had shared became grist for Jake's burgeoning writing career.

"So what new story are you into now?" Nog asked, swallowing the last squiggling tube grub. "Going to write about how I saved Earth from the Changelings?"

"My father and Odo did that," Jake replied.

"With *my* help. I was the one who made them realize the plot was actually coming from inside Starfleet."

"You did help," Jake had to admit. "But there are still Changelings on Earth."

"Only one or two," came a deep voice with an Irish brogue from behind them.

They turned to find *Deep Space Nine's* chief of engineering, Miles O'Brien, standing there. Like Jake, O'Brien had remained behind on Earth while the rest of the station's contingent, including his father, had returned. O'Brien was overseeing repairs to the *Defiant* and would take the starship back to *Deep Space Nine* when they were complete. Jake would return with him.

But first, there was another mission to be accomplished. O'Brien had promised to deliver something to one of Jadzia Dax's former teachers who was working on an advanced physics research project in France. He invited Jake and Nog to come along—an offer they readily accepted.

"I can't wait to see Paris," Jake said.

"We'll beam over there as soon as I eat," O'Brien said, sitting down. "I've heard your grandfather serves the best Cajun crawfish in New Orleans."

"I won't deny that." Jake's grandfather, Joseph Sisko, had come out of the kitchen with a platter of grits for the next table. He smiled at the trio as he passed. Jake loved his grandfather, who was well into his seventies but moved with the energy and enthusiasm of a man half his age, but he hated it when the old man put him to work in the kitchen.

Although he enjoyed preparing meals for himself and his father on *Deep Space Nine,* Jake was of the opinion that cooking without a replicator was something they did back in the Dark Ages.

"Cooking is not something to be relegated to machines," his grandfather argued. "It needs a human touch."

That human touch usually meant Jake ended up chopping vegetables in the restaurant's kitchen or waiting tables, neither of which made his list of the top ten things to do while on Earth. But going to Paris, now that was another matter.

"I've been reading up on France," Nog said. "It sounds really interesting."

"It is," Jake said. "They call Paris the City of Light. Artists and poets from all over the Federation still go there for inspiration."

"I'm afraid we won't be there long enough for much inspiration," O'Brien said. "I'm just going as a favor to Dax. Promised to deliver this bonsai tree from Iszm in person to her old Starfleet professor, Jonathan Vance."

"I've heard of him," Nog said. "He used to teach

advanced spatial physics at the Academy, until he left to do research on temporal anomalies. He's a brilliant scientist."

"I suspect he is," O'Brien said as he tasted his crawfish breakfast. "Me, I'm more of a tinkerer than a thinker."

Jake looked at the tiny tree that was Dax's gift to her former Starfleet mentor. Or one of her mentors. Dax was a Trill who had shared the lives of eight hosts—Jadzia being the most recent—so she/he probably had several mentors in past lives.

The tree was a miniature oak from the planet Iszm, which was famous throughout the quadrant for its exotic plants. O'Brien carried the tree in a small translucent stasis field. While the oaks on Iszm grew to massive proportions under the planet's light gravity, this oak was barely nine inches tall. Yet it was perfect in every way and had the gnarled look of a tree that had lived for generations.

"Beautiful, isn't it?" O'Brien said, with the same admiring tone Jake had heard him use when describing a well-running turbo generator. "I was going to clone it in the replicator for Keiko, but she said it was unique and shouldn't be artificially duplicated."

"A wise decision," Joseph Sisko said as he joined them. "There are things that aren't meant to be replicated."

"You may be right," O'Brien said. "But I wouldn't mind having the recipe for this sauce programmed into the station's system."

"Sorry," Joseph said. "I never let my recipes be replicated. I'm old-fashioned that way. Besides, the duplicates never taste quite as good as the original."

Once Jake thought that his grandfather's ideas were like the old man, out of date and old-fashioned. But now he was beginning to see their wisdom. He was right that one couldn't replicate creativity.

The older he got, the more Jake grew to appreciate his grandfather.

After they finished their lunch, the trio said goodbye to Joseph Sisko and strolled along the canal to the neighborhood transporter station. It was drizzling, and a wet, gray mist hung over the city. From previous visits to his grandfather, Jake knew that June in New Orleans was often damp and chilly.

"I hope the weather's better in Paris," Nog said as they entered the warmth of the public transporter station.

Jake didn't really care what it was like. He was just looking forward to being in the City of Light. He only hoped he wouldn't be disappointed.

CHAPTER 2

Earth, Paris, Same Day

He wasn't. Jake found Paris in early summer to be a symphony for the senses. This was a city that had beckoned to writers, from Victor Hugo to Ernest Hemingway, and most recently the Vulcan poet Olvek, who had settled here in the last century and still worked in a loft somewhere on the Left Bank.

It was early evening in this part of the world. One of those warm, misty summer evenings in Paris when the air was filled with the sweet fragrance of chestnut trees, while a hint of approaching thunder hung on the horizon.

They arrived in the city at a busy transporter station near the Seine. The river, which was once dangerously close to extinction from pollution, had been reborn and was now a lovely blue ribbon that snaked its way through the city. Jake imagined the river had been like this two thousand years ago when the city was still only a minor fishing village occupied by the Romans.

Dominating the city was the famous symbol of Paris, the Eiffel Tower. It rose above the nearby rooftops like the spidery frame of an uncompleted pyramid. Actually, Jake knew, this was not the original tower. That had been destroyed in the twenty-first century during the Third World War. But the new one had been painstakingly re-created from the original blueprints.

The Eiffel Tower was such an icon for the city, Jake found it hard to believe that after it had been built for a world's fair in 1889, many of the French elite considered it ugly and demanded it be torn down. Fortunately that didn't happen, and the tower had remained ever since as a magnet that attracted people from all over the quadrant to Paris.

Their destination was the laboratory where Vance worked. It was located in a research park northwest of the city. They could have beamed directly there, but this was Paris, so they opted to take a hovercab and see the sights along the way.

That might have been a mistake. The driver zoomed in, around, and over the twisting streets of the city at near warp speed, leaving little opportunity for any sightseeing.

"French cab drivers haven't changed in a millennium," O'Brien remarked when they arrived at their destination.

The Advanced Physics Research Center was a cluster of seven white buildings, all of them three stories in height and looking exactly alike. The buildings were ringed by a wide park of green grass and chestnut trees. This could have been any industrial center on any planet in the Federation—except for the security.

There were no fences around the center, but it was totally enclosed in a force field, similar to those used on a starship for defense.

Nothing short of a salvo of heavy-duty photon torpedoes would disturb the occupants, Jake thought as the Starfleet duty officer scanned their identity badges and ushered them through the entrance gate.

"Professor Vance is expecting you," the officer said, handing them a small PADD that showed them the way. The PADD was imprinted with a security alarm that would activate if they took any unwarranted detours.

"Whatever the professor's involved in, it must be important," Nog said as they rode a slidewalk to the sixth building.

"Temporal displacement," Professor Vance explained after everyone had been properly introduced. "In layman terms, time travel."

"The control of time is more important than the control of space," added the professor's assistant, Pierre, a tall, thin Frenchman who was the direct opposite of the short, squat Vance.

"Perhaps," was Professor Vance's only comment. He seemed much more interested at the moment in examining the bonsai tree that O'Brien had delivered than in discussing the physical or political aspects of time travel.

It was Pierre who showed Jake and Nog around the lab while Vance and O'Brien remained behind to discuss botanical pursuits.

"I've studied temporal disturbances at the Academy," Nog said as they looked around what Pierre called the "time lab." It reminded Jake of an inactive holosuite. There was very little in the room itself, except for a single work table and a control panel located in the wall next to the door.

"But they require a tremendous amount of energy," Jake commented. He had done his own reading. "Starships have broken through the time barrier, but only when traveling at hyperwarp velocities."

"Energy is indeed the key," Pierre replied. "With a power source great enough, virtually anything is possible."

"So where does the energy come from?" Nog asked.

"Ah, that's our little secret." Pierre smiled and stepped over to the control panel. He punched in a code, and there was a low whirring sound, like the Cardassian generators that powered *Deep Space Nine*. "Actually, the secret belongs to Professor Vance, and he's shared it with no one—not even me."

"He's found a new source of power?" Jake wondered.

TRAPPED IN TIME

"Perhaps," Pierre answered. "Or maybe he's just found a way to amplify the current sources." Pierre tapped the control panel. "All I know is that the power that pours through these circuits is equivalent to the amount of energy generated at a star's core."

Jake and Nog were impressed. Then they turned their attention to the center of the lab and were even more impressed.

A pulsating cube materialized in the center of the room. It floated about half a meter off the floor and began to grow until it was the size of a door. It was originally a blurred yellow in color, but as it took on more definition, it became a dark orange shade. That was the cube's boundaries. Inside the cube there was—*nothing.*

Not just something that couldn't be seen, but *nothing,* as if the interior was a gateway that led to—*nowhere.*

"We call it the portal," Pierre explained.

"Portal means it links to somewhere," Jake said. "Where does it go?"

"Anywhere and any*when* you want to go," Pierre said. "At present there is enough power to travel back through several centuries of Earth's history."

"Can you go into the future?" Nog asked.

"No. The way the professor explains it is that at any fixed moment in time, there are an infinite number of possible futures. Each choice made in a fixed moment determines what the future will be. To travel into a place that—for us—does not yet exist and could have a hundred billion possible forms requires far more energy than we've been able to tap into so far."

"Perhaps it can't be done," Jake said. "Maybe we can only go back in time."

"And change the future," Nog added, thinking of the possibilities. For a brief moment he was more Ferengi entrepreneur than Starfleet cadet.

"That is the dilemma we find ourselves in," Professor Vance said as he entered the room, accompanied by O'Brien. "Unfortunately, the ability to reshape destiny has always appealed to humankind."

"To play God can be very attractive," Jake admitted as he considered all the potentials of the professor's invention—for good or evil.

"You mean you could actually go back and change the past to create a different future?" O'Brien asked.

"It's possible, but more difficult than you might imagine." The professor paused, then continued. "Think of time as a river. Tossing a pebble, even a large boulder, into the river will do little to alter its course. But if you block the river at a strategic narrow point, perhaps felling a tree to create a dam, then you might affect the flow—and change the course of the river."

"Sounds like this could be very dangerous in the wrong hands," O'Brien commented.

"Yes. It would be." The professor took out a small remote device from his pocket. "Which is why I've got the only control device, and it's specifically coded to my unique retinal scan pattern. Even if it were stolen, it couldn't be used by anyone else." The professor put the device away. "That's how it will remain until the Federation determines what shall become of my invention."

It was night when Jake, Nog, and O'Brien left the building. There was a sliver of a moon on the horizon which occasionally peeked through the clouds. A brisk wind had picked up and stirred the trees. Somewhere in the distance was a bright flash, followed shortly by the low rumble of thunder.

"Storm coming," O'Brien commented.

Jake and Nog didn't notice the distant storm. Their heads were still swimming with all the possibilities of time travel. They didn't notice the man hurrying toward them along the slidewalk—until he collided with them.

"Sorry," Jake apologized, helping the man to his feet. Then he froze as saw who the man was.

"Pierre," Nog said as he, too, recognized the face.

"Do I know you?" Pierre asked. It was apparent that he didn't know either of them.

"We were just talking with you," Jake replied. "In the lab."

"Impossible," Pierre said. "I spent the day in Provence."

"But, if you weren't here—who was it that was with Professor Vance?" Nog wondered.

"One guess," O'Brien said. He had already turned and was heading back toward the building. "Only one species could perform such a perfect impersonation."

Jake knew what O'Brien was thinking and spoke the dreaded word aloud: "Changeling!"

CHAPTER 3

Earth, Paris, Same Day

While they rushed back to the laboratory, Pierre explained that he had been called away on urgent family business early that morning. He had beamed to a small village in France's Provence region. But there had been no urgency, and no one admitted to making the call. Pierre suspected it had been a prank.

A strange power outage in the village had prevented him from using the transporter facility to beam to Paris, so he had taken a train back to the city. He thought the whole thing was strange but didn't consider it threatening—until now.

The professor's lab was located on the third level of the building, but the lift was stuck between the second and third levels. Not a good sign.

"We'll take the stairs," O'Brien shouted.

Jake, Nog, and Pierre followed the chief engineer

up the winding stairwell. Jake wasn't sure what he expected to find when they burst into the lab—but it wasn't what did greet them.

"Professor?" O'Brien asked as they found Vance hunched over something on the table. Jake couldn't quite see what it was that the professor was tinkering with, and as he turned it was shielded from their view by his body.

"Pierre. I thought you'd left. And Chief O'Brien, what brings you back? Did you forget something?"

"Where's your assistant?" O'Brien asked.

"Why, he's standing next to you," Professor Vance replied, confusion obvious in his voice and expression.

"We mean the *real* Pierre," Nog said.

"What're you talking about?"

"You two try to explain," O'Brien said to Jake and Nog, then he turned and ran out of the lab. Pierre hesitated a moment, then followed O'Brien.

"All right," Professor Vance said, looking at Jake and Nog. "Please tell me what is going on."

While Nog told the professor that they thought his assistant was really a Changeling, Jake was noticing the table. He saw what Vance had been working on: the remote time control device. Then Jake noticed that the control panel monitor was blinking.

"You've activated the time portal," Jake realized.

"Well done, young Sisko," Professor Vance acknowledged. "You'd make a great detective."

Jake began to put things together in his mind. His intuition was carrying him toward a conclusion at warp speed. "I'll bet O'Brien doesn't find the other Pierre."

Nog looked at his friend. "What are you thinking?"

"That the fake Pierre no longer exists. That the Changeling has taken on a new identity." Jake looked at Professor Vance. "I'll bet the reason the lift is stuck between levels is that someone is trapped inside it—the real Professor Vance."

"Quite a piece of deduction." Professor Vance smiled and stepped over to the table. He picked up the remote device. "Unfortunately—you're exactly right."

Vance entered a code into the remote device. "It's easy to impersonate someone outwardly. But much more difficult to copy a simple retinal scan, even for a short period." Now he pressed the activation key. "So you won't mind if I cut this short."

Directly behind where Professor Vance was standing, Jake saw the temporal portal materialize—first as a small pulsating dot that hung in midair, then rapidly expanding until it became a human-sized rectangle. "He's opening the portal!"

Nog and Jake moved toward the professor, then stopped when Vance pulled out a phaser from beneath his jacket. "Sorry, I really do have to go. Things to do, places to be, history to change."

Vance was almost at the portal when the lab door

opened. O'Brien entered. Right behind him Jake could see Pierre helping a wobbly Professor Vance—the real professor.

"You must stop him!" the real professor shouted. "The damage he could do in the past . . . might change the course of history."

"I certainly hope so," the other Vance said. Then he aimed the phaser and fired.

The phaser blast wasn't aimed at any of the people in the room, but rather at the control panel on the wall. "I'd rather no one followed me."

The portal flickered for a moment, but the Changeling Vance adjusted the remote device, and the portal stabilized. "Now I have the only key that unlocks the door to the past."

With that, he turned and stepped into the portal. As he entered the swirling vortex, Vance suddenly morphed into a golden gelatinous state.

And then he was gone.

"Definitely a Changeling!" O'Brien exclaimed.

"Where's he going?" Jake asked.

"Wherever—or whenever—it is, we've got to stop him!" Nog yelled, and he ran toward the portal.

"Nog! Wait!" Jake shouted. But it was too late. The Ferengi had already entered the vortex.

Jake hesitated only a moment. The portal was shrinking. It would close in another moment—with Nog and the Changeling trapped on the other side. Jake had no idea where he was about to go, but he knew he couldn't desert his best friend. He ran into the vortex—and vanished.

O'Brien did not hesitate even a moment. The two boys had followed the Changeling to the stars knew where and left him with no choice. They were his responsibility.

In the final instant before the portal collapsed, O'Brien leaped into the swirling vortex.

Behind him, in the lab, the portal closed. Ahead of him there was a dizzying display of bright light. He fell forward, tumbling down through the void toward the light. Wherever—and whenever—they were going, there was no turning back now.

CHAPTER 4

Earth, Stardate Unknown

Wherever they were, it certainly wasn't Paris. They might not even be in France anymore.

Jake was having second thoughts about leaping before looking. But it was too late for that now. He looked over his shoulder in time to see O'Brien follow him through the temporal portal just before it closed.

"Well, lads," O'Brien said, echoing the thoughts of all of them. "Wherever we are, we're here for the duration."

"How are we going to get back?" Nog asked.

"We'll need to find the Changeling and get the control unit," Jake answered, realizing as he spoke that it wasn't going to be easy.

"First things first," O'Brien said. "Right now we need to know where in blazes we are."

Jake looked around. Wherever they were, it was night, and it was cold. There was no moon or stars overhead, only a dark cloud cover that obscured the sky. It wasn't raining, but the damp ground informed Jake that it had rained not long before. And, from the damp feel of air, might start again at any moment.

"We need to find shelter," O'Brien said.

"But what about the Changeling?" Nog asked.

"We'll never locate him in the dark," O'Brien answered. Already he was looking around for someplace to go that would get them out of the cold.

"Besides," Jake added, "he could have changed into anyone. There's no way we'd recognize him."

"Great," Nog said. "We're stuck who-knows-where looking for who-knows-who."

Jake decided that this was not the appropriate moment to remind his Ferengi friend that it was his impulsive action that had landed them there. "When we find out where we are, then we'll be able to figure out what critical moment in time the Changeling plans to alter. And that should lead us to him."

"Unless he's already accomplished his mission," Nog said. "The future might have already been changed."

"We can only hope that hasn't happened," Jake said. "Besides, we've only been here a few minutes, which means so has the Changeling. History isn't that easy to rewrite."

Nog was rubbing his ears. He looked even colder

than Jake felt. This was going to be a very long night if they had to spend it outside on wet ground.

"Over there." O'Brien was pointing to a building in the distance.

"What is it?" Jake asked.

"Looks like a barn," O'Brien replied. "Should give us some shelter."

While they walked across a soggy field to the barn, Jake looked around at their surroundings. It was dark, but the absence of a lot of structures seemed to indicate that they were in a rural area.

The ground squished like a sponge underfoot, Jake's boots scrunching as he walked. They were crossing an open field. It gave him the impression of being on a farm. As they neared the barn, he could see another building some distance beyond. It might be the farmhouse.

"Maybe we should go to that house," Jake suggested.

O'Brien shook his head. "Not until we have a better idea of where—and when—we are."

There was no lock on the door to the barn, but the door creaked in protest as O'Brien forced it open. Jake was certain that someone must have heard them, but he looked back at the farmhouse and saw no lights coming on or doors opening.

Inside Jake saw that it was indeed a barn. Except there were no animals, although there were pens that might have housed a cow or a horse. In the darkness it

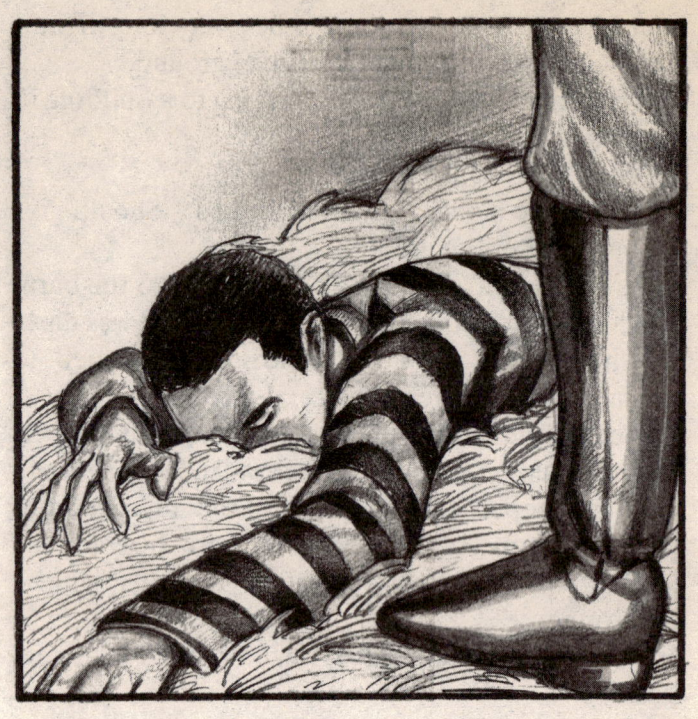

was hard to tell, but he had the distinct impression that the building had not been occupied in some time.

"Do you have any idea what time period this is?" Nog asked.

"Hard to tell," O'Brien said. "Based on the harnesses and tools, it could be anywhere from the late eighteen hundreds to the middle of the twenty-first century."

Jake rummaged around and found a spot next to

the wall and sat down. He was tired, more so than he had realized. "We can figure it out in the morning."

Nog opened his mouth, about to complain, but O'Brien interrupted. "Jake's right. We can't go running around in the dark. Come morning, when we're rested, we'll make a plan."

Good idea, Jake thought, as he leaned back against the boards. *We need a plan.* As he drifted off into a fitful sleep, he tried to formulate one in his mind. Often, when he had reached a writer's block where he had no idea what to do next, he would stop. That night he would repeat the problem as he fell asleep, and often the answer would be waiting for him when he woke up in the morning.

But if his subconscious had been working on a plan for this situation, it vanished—as Jake was suddenly jerked out of his slumber by the sound of strange voices.

He felt something cold and hard against his ribs. He tried to push it away, but the prodding became more insistent and the voices louder.

Jake opened his eyes and looked up to see a soldier in a strange uniform staring down at him. The man was speaking in a foreign tongue and jabbing at him with the deadly barrel of a rifle.

CHAPTER 5

Earth, France, 20th Century

Jake froze as he looked into the barrel of the rifle. Wherever they were, the natives were definitely not friendly.

He looked at the uniform of the man holding the rifle. It was obviously military, but beyond that he had no idea which army this soldier belonged to.

"German," O'Brien said. "They're Germans."

Jake turned to see O'Brien being forced up against the wall by two of the soldiers. There were four in all. The one guarding O'Brien, the one standing on top of him, and two others looking for whoever else might be in the barn.

"I recognize the uniforms. We're in the middle of the twentieth century—the Second World War." Before O'Brien could elaborate, one of the soldiers clubbed him hard in the stomach with the butt of his rifle and sent the chief engineer sagging to his knees.

The German soldiers were not in a mood to discuss things. *We have to escape,* Jake thought. *But how?*

Suddenly Jake was aware that something was missing here. Or rather some*one* was missing.

Where's Nog?

Before Jake could consider the whereabouts of his missing friend, the roof fell in. Literally.

Loose boards and boxes tumbled down from the barn's loft on top of the German soldiers. One of them was hit in the shoulder by a plank and fell to the ground. The two soldiers who had been searching the barn scrambled to get out of the way of the falling debris.

Jake looked up to see Nog, who had been hiding in the loft, leap down. He landed on top of the soldier guarding Jake, knocking them both to the ground.

O'Brien seized the moment of confusion. He kicked the legs out from under the soldier who had been guarding him, grabbing his rifle in the process.

On the floor Nog wrestled with the soldier, and Jake ran to help his friend.

The other two Germans had started to recover from their confusion, and there was a tense moment when it was uncertain who held the balance of power.

Then O'Brien fired a warning shot from the rifle.

"Everybody freeze!" O'Brien shouted at the Germans.

Without hesitation, two of the soldiers bolted out the door. Jake grabbed the rifle that the soldier who was wrestling with Nog had dropped.

"OK, Nog! I've got his weapon." Jake looked at the strange rifle in his hands. "Not that I'm sure how to use it."

"Point it and pull the trigger," O'Brien said. "It's not a phaser, so be careful. It packs a kick—and can inflict a lot of damage to your target." O'Brien looked at the German soldier he had turned the tables on as he made that last comment.

"You are not French," the soldier said as he stared at O'Brien. He spoke English quite well. "You are British."

"Close, but no Bajoran orb. I'm Irish. And proud of it."

Now the soldier took his first good look at Nog. His eyes widened. "That one is . . . strange."

"He's—ah . . . from the provinces," Jake tried to explain. Even in the urgency of their situation, he knew it could create a problem if enough people suspected there was an extraterrestrial in twentieth-century France. He wasn't certain if people were into UFOs in this time period. "He was . . . *deformed* at birth. That's why he looks like that."

"Deformed." Nog was incensed. "I'm as handsome a Ferengi as you'll find."

"Ferengi?" the soldier questioned.

"Family name," O'Brien explained. Then he turned to Jake and Nog. "Interesting situation we have here.

Two German prisoners, and no real idea where we are."

"Ask him," Jake said as he pointed to the soldier who spoke English.

"Where are we?" O'Brien asked the soldier. The soldier hesitated. O'Brien pushed the barrel of the rifle into his chest. "If that's not a military secret?"

The soldier hesitated another moment, then answered, "This is Normandy."

"Normandy." O'Brien repeated the word, then asked the soldier, "What's the date?" The soldier was again hesitant, this time out of obvious confusion. O'Brien prodded him again. "The date?"

But before the soldier could reply, there was noise outside the barn. Voices—and something else—were moving toward them.

"Sounds like the ones who escaped have returned—and brought their friends," Jake said.

"What's that noise?" Nog asked. "It sounds like a machine."

"Bashir and I have played enough holosuite war games to recognize that sound in our sleep," O'Brien replied. "It's a German tank!"

Nog stepped over to the barn door and looked outside. "And it's a big one!"

"It would be best if you surrendered peacefully," the German soldier said, his courage suddenly raised by the imminent arrival of his friends.

"Don't think so," O'Brien said. "Close the door, Nog. And bolt it."

Nog quickly obeyed. There was no lock, but he grabbed a heavy plank. Jake came over and helped to put the plank in place. They positioned it to hold the door shut, although Jake thought it was doubtful it would do much to keep out the approaching tank. He had caught a brief glimpse of the tank while Nog was swinging the door shut. It was very big.

"Now what do we do?" Nog wondered.

O'Brien motioned for Jake and Nog to climb up to the loft. "There's a window up there that leads out the back."

Jake looked at the two soldiers. "They'll give us away."

"No, they won't." For a moment Jake thought O'Brien might shoot them. This was a war they were in the middle of, after all. But killing anyone, even an enemy who would probably not show the same reluctance, was not something that he wanted to witness, much less participate in.

To Jake's relief, O'Brien instead used the butt of the rifle to knock them both unconscious. "Sorry about that. You're going to have a whopper of a headache, but it's a lot better than being dead." O'Brien looked at Jake and Nog, who had paused near the top of the ladder leading up to the loft. "We have to be careful what we do here. These soldiers may not be destined to die in the war, so killing them—or anyone in this time period—might unintentionally change the future."

Behind them the voices and the noise of the approaching tank were growing ominously louder as they neared the barn. Quickly O'Brien scrambled up the ladder.

"We have to move fast," O'Brien said as he moved to the window. "The Germans will have this place surrounded in a moment. We'll be trapped."

The window was small, barely large enough to squeeze through. But that was not what worried Jake. The ground below them seemed a long way down. *That* worried Jake.

"The ground is wet and spongy," O'Brien said. "We should be OK. Land like a paratrooper. When you hit the ground, let your body absorb the impact, and roll."

"Just like Academy basic training." Nog smiled and went out through the window.

Jake saw the Ferengi hit the ground, double up, and roll exactly as O'Brien had instructed. Then Nog was up on his feet and waved to his friend to follow.

There was an instant of uncertainty. It was the second time that evening that Jake had followed Nog into the unknown.

Then he was out the window and falling through space. The ground seemed to be even farther away than it looked. Jake hit the ground hard. It was a *lot* harder than he had imagined. His feet collapsed under him, and he sprawled rather than rolled with the impact. The air rushed out of his stomach as if he had been punched.

Nog ran over and helped Jake to his feet. He was

wobbly, and it took a moment for him to regain his balance. Then they looked up in time to see O'Brien start to follow.

Suddenly there was an incredible roar. The German tank must have fired a cannon blast at the front of the barn. The whole structure shook violently—sending O'Brien crashing down toward the ground out of control.

O'Brien fell through the air, hitting the ground off balance and falling sideways. He lay there motionless for a long moment as Jake and Nog rushed to help him.

"Watch that first step," O'Brien mumbled as Jake tried to help the chief to his feet. Suddenly O'Brien winced with pain and fell backward.

"What's wrong?" Jake asked, almost afraid to hear the answer.

"My ankle," O'Brien said, his eyes glazed with the obvious pain he was feeling. "Twisted . . . maybe broken."

"We can carry you," Jake said. He and Nog tried to lift O'Brien.

"No," O'Brien commanded. "I can't run. And if you carry me, I'll slow you down—and we'll all be caught."

"We can't leave you," Jake said.

"You have to." O'Brien was not asking them, he was giving them an order. In the background the voices were growing louder. The Germans were inside the barn, and they'd be out there in a moment. Jake knew there was no time to debate the course of action. He also knew O'Brien was right.

"Come on, Nog," Jake said to the Ferengi. "It's up to us to find the Changeling."

Nog started to protest, but he, too, realized that this was their only course of action. He looked at O'Brien. "We'll be back for you."

"I know you will. Now get going."

So they ran.

The ground was wet and marshy, which made running hard, but it also muffled their footsteps. The cloudy night hid the moon, making it difficult for them to be spotted by any pursuing Germans.

They were certain they were being chased. Jake could only hope they had enough of a head start to elude their pursuers.

"Any idea where we're going?" Nog whispered as they ran.

"None," Jake answered in his own breathless whisper. He didn't know how long they had been running, but his lungs were straining to catch a breath, and his legs were running on sheer adrenaline. Maybe they had outdistanced the Germans and could stop, but he was afraid to take the chance. But he didn't know how much longer he could keep up this pace.

"We have to stop," Nog said after they had run a short distance farther.

"We can't . . ." Jake started to protest, but his exhausted legs were in agreement with Nog.

They stopped.

All around them the night was silent, except for the chirping of insects and the occasional hooting of a distant owl. There was no sound of voices, German or otherwise.

"If we keep going, we might run into another German patrol," Nog said.

Jake knew he was right. He remembered his history. This was Occupied France during Earth's Second World War. The enemy was everywhere. They needed daylight. They needed to know exactly where they were. And they needed a plan. Things were rapidly deteriorating from bad to worse.

"I'm wet." Nog's complaint suddenly caused Jake to realize that his feet were ankle deep in water. They had stopped running just in time, or they would have plunged straight into a marsh. "And I've lost my commbadge."

"Doesn't matter," Jake replied.

"How will we find Chief O'Brien without it?" Nog asked as he felt around in the dark water without success.

"We won't find him *with* it," Jake replied. "This is nineteen forty-four. The nearest global computer network is several hundred years away. In this time period, a commbadge is as useful as a radio is to a caveman."

"Maybe so," Nog admitted. "But it is Starfleet property, and they'll charge me for it."

"Right now we have more urgent problems," Jake said. "We need to move to higher ground." He looked up at the night sky. The dark clouds were beginning to turn from black to gray. Dawn was coming. They had to find a safe place.

There was a thick clump of trees not far away. The ground was still damp and soggy, but the foliage was dense enough to shelter them from prying eyes. Or so they hoped.

Jake tried to sleep, or at least nap. He was only partially successful. He had been on camping weekends several times with his father, both on Mars and on Earth, and that helped. But trying to remain alert to any unusual sound in a place where most of the natural sounds were unusual to him made it difficult. Finally, after several futile attempts, he did manage to doze.

Morning arrived too soon. The sky was still overcast, and the clouds were painted with several variations of gray. It mirrored Jake's mood as he sat up.

Nog was equally pessimistic. "We have a problem. A really big problem."

Jake was well aware of that. He had been trying to formulate a plan, or at least a course of action. But their plight did seem pretty hopeless.

"We don't know where the Changeling is. We don't know where Chief O'Brien is." Jake listed their problems. "We don't even know where *we* are."

"And I'm freezing," Nog added.

Jake was cold, too. Very cold. The clothes they were wearing were not intended for survival in the outdoors. At least Nog's Academy uniform was woven with a fabric that retained body warmth in cold weather and expelled it during hot. But even it was not designed for these kinds of circumstances. And Jake's clothing provided even less protection against the morning chill.

"I think—" Jake started to suggest what they should do next, but Nog held up a hand to silence him. Jake could see Nog's large ears quivering. One advantage they did have was Nog's keen Ferengi sense of hearing.

"Someone's coming," Nog whispered.

"Where?" Jake asked, keeping his voice low.

Nog pointed out in the direction of the marsh and the deep lake beyond. "That way. A boat."

Jake listened. At first there was nothing, then he began to hear it. Someone rowing a boat. He could hear the sound of the oars as they stroked through the water.

"Germans?" Jake said softly, wondering if they had been discovered.

Jake and Nog tried to become invisible, staying low and blending into the foliage as best they could, as the boat drew nearer. They were some distance from the edge of the marsh and, they hoped, would not be seen by those in the boat.

Which appeared to be the case as the boat moved past them and farther down the marsh. Crouched down in the brush, Jake was unable to see if German soldiers were in the boat. Perhaps it was only a local fisherman out to catch breakfast.

TRAPPED IN TIME

So intent where they on not being heard or seen that neither Jake nor Nog was aware of someone else moving toward them from the opposite direction—until it was too late.

"Hold." The single word was sharp as a knife.

Jake bolted up from the brush and turned in time to see something rushing toward his head. There was an instant of blinding pain, and then he mercifully fell into unconsciousness.

CHAPTER 6

Earth, Occupied France, Normandy, 1944

Stars swirled in Jake's head. Strange nebulas and distant novas. Slowly, relentlessly, he was being drawn toward a gigantic black hole. He tried to retreat, but there was no escape. The overwhelming pull of gravity sucked him into the darkness. The stars vanished, and he was falling . . . falling . . . falling through the absolute darkness. Was he dying?

Then, up ahead, there was a pinpoint of bright light. He was falling toward the light. It grew and grew . . . until it surrounded him.

And then Jake opened his eyes.

The light was not all around him but coming from a bare bulb that hung from the ceiling above.

Jake's head felt as if it were splitting, but he was alive.

"Feeling better?" The voice that greeted him was soft and gentle.

Slowly, because his head really hurt, Jake twisted his neck. The face he saw next to him—he was lying on a small bed—did not belong to the voice. It was a man, old and weathered, with a stubble beard that was as rough and untended as the man.

"That's Uncle Maurice." The gentle voice whispering in his ear was coming from the other side of the bed. Jake slowly turned in that direction. The voice he had heard belonged to a young woman, perhaps a year younger—or older—than he was. Jake was really bad at determining ages, especially women's.

"My name is Brigitte." She was speaking English but with an obvious French accent. She had long black hair and a pleasant smile, but Jake could sense an underlying strength and determination.

Jake asked the obvious. "Where am I?"

"Nous demandons les questions." The voice came from the other side of the room. He was a stocky middle-aged Frenchman seated in a chair. He was also smiling, but there was something about his voice. Jake had the impression that it would be better to be this man's friend than his enemy.

Jake looked to Brigitte for a translation. "That is Monsieur Jean. He says that he will ask the questions." She leaned closer to Jake and added in a soft voice, "It would be best if you answered."

The man named Monsieur Jean was looking at Jake in a way that made him feel as if he were an Orion tree toad about to be bisected. He didn't like the feeling any more than he thought the toad did.

"You are American?" Monsieur Jean asked, this time in a halting English that Jake understood.

Jake hesitated a moment, then nodded. It was a logical reply, and one he hoped the man would accept. He hoped these people were part of the French

Resistance, freedom fighters against the Germans. If not, they were back to square one.

"What are you doing here?"

Jake hesitated again. This question was more difficult. "My friend and I . . ." He had no idea where Nog was and could only hope that he was all right. "We became lost."

"You certainly did." Monsieur Jean let out a loud laugh that eased the tension—for a moment. "Your friend. Tell me about him. About the strange one."

That was the biggest challenge. Jake couldn't tell him the truth, and to pretend Nog was French wasn't going to work here. "He is . . . he has a disease. It deformed him," Jake said finally.

Jake could see Monsieur Jean considering this. It was probably a rational explanation for Nog.

"But his condition is stable . . . and not contagious," Jake added quickly.

"That is good," Monsieur Jean said.

"Where is Nog?" Jake asked.

"He is safe," Brigitte whispered to Jake. "In the cellar."

"Yes," Monsieur Jean said. "He is safe. You are both safe—for the moment."

Monsieur Jean rose and went to the door. He started to open it, then looked over at Uncle Maurice, who had sat like a statue and remained silent through all of this. "Put him with his friend," Monsieur Jean said. "Make sure they are guarded, until we decide their fate."

Jake didn't like that "decide their fate" remark. It was apparent that Monsieur Jean did not really accept Jake's story, but at least he didn't consider them enemies—not yet.

Uncle Maurice helped Jake up from the bed. Jake was wobbly and still a bit dizzy. He wondered if his head looked as bad as it felt. He reached up and felt bandages on his forehead and a sharp rush of pain from the pressure of his fingers.

"The skin was broken. I bandaged it. It will hurt, but you will live," Brigitte said.

But for how long? Jake wondered as he was led out of the room. This was not going well at all. He only hoped O'Brien was having better luck, wherever he was.

Miles O'Brien, chief of operations of the Bajoran space station *Deep Space Nine,* was not having much luck. He felt things were not going well at all. He found himself sitting alone in a small room with an aching ankle and wondering if he would ever again see that station or his wife and daughter again.

Once, when he had been framed, captured, and put on trial by the Cardassians, he had harbored similar thoughts. But then, at least, he had the support and help of Captain Sisko and the rest of the station. Now his only hope of rescue lay in the stealth and cunning of two teenage boys who were as lost in this time and place as he was.

Normally full of self-confidence, O'Brien was a man who had used ingenuity and whatever tools were at hand to return control from chaos while serving as ptransporter chief on the *U.S.S. Enterprise* and now chief of operations on *Deep Space Nine*. But now he found himself in the unsettling position of having run out of innovations and resources.

O'Brien noticed that his commbadge was missing. He remembered that the war had been going on for a long time, and Germany was desperate for metal to melt down for machines and weapons. Obviously it had been appropriated for that purpose. Which was just as well. In this time period a commbadge from the twenty-fourth century was meaningless, but if it survived a century or two, some bright young engineer might get ideas.

But there was nothing he could do about that. All he could do was sit in this tiny, windowless room and wait for what would come next.

He didn't have long to wait.

The door opened, and a tall man in the uniform of a German officer entered. There was an armed guard stationed behind him. The officer waved his hand, and the guard closed the door.

"I am Colonel Kruger. Sorry about the lack of accommodations," the colonel said in perfect English with a thick German accent. "This building had once been a hotel before we appropriated it for the war

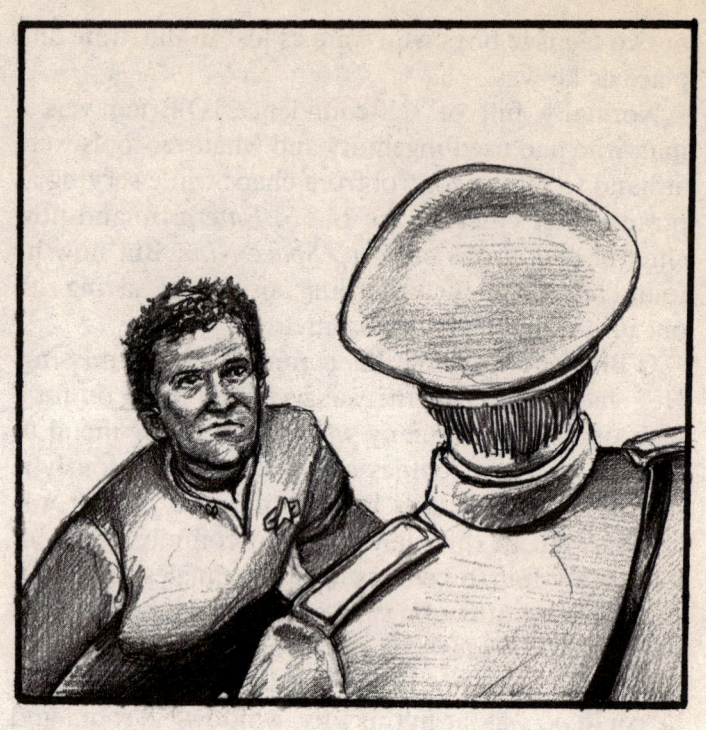

effort. This maintenance room is the only holding cell we have."

O'Brien remained silent. He looked at the colonel and tried to size him up. The words that came to mind were *stiff* and *stoic*. O'Brien had the sense of a career military man who played his cards very close to his chest. He was also sure the Germans would consider him a spy, and he knew what they did to spies. This was war, and there would not even be the pretense of a trial.

"Your ankle is not broken." The colonel seemed genuinely interested in O'Brien's health.

"Not broken. But it sure hurts."

"Sorry that we cannot provide medicine for your pain." The colonel sat down in a chair across from O'Brien. "But until we determine your status, such luxuries are unavailable."

"You mean, if you're going to shoot me, there's no sense in wasting medicine." It was not a question.

"Something like that." There was a long moment as the colonel looked at O'Brien. Finally he spoke. "You are going to die, Chief O'Brien. It is a pity, and unnecessary if you had not been so reckless as to follow me."

O'Brien blinked. This colonel knew who he was. *He must be the Changeling!* This was the identity he had assumed.

"You may be wondering what happened to the real Colonel Kruger. Unfortunately, an accident. Caused not by me but by the French Resistance. His body will not be discovered until several days from now. By then, I will have no further use for this body."

"I see you've done your homework," O'Brien said.

"Quite thoroughly, I assure you."

"But you won't get away with it."

Colonel Kruger smiled. "Such a weak response. I expected more. Or, perhaps, you're trying to trick me into telling you what my plan is."

"I think I already know that," O'Brien said.

"Yes, I suppose you do. This is a critical time in the history of Earth. Had the war been won by the Germans, the future of your planet would be much more orderly."

"You Changelings love order, don't you?" O'Brien said. "Even at the price of individual freedom."

"Freedom." Colonel Kruger repeated the word. "You humans place too much emphasis on its value. When we brought order out of chaos in the Gamma Quadrant through the Dominion, many lost their freedom, but they gained stability and prosperity in return."

"Under the yoke of your Jem'Hadar shock troops. The people of Earth aren't going to submit so easily—to you or the Nazis." But even as he spoke the words, O'Brien was very much afraid that the future the Changeling envisioned might come to pass.

CHAPTER 7

Earth, Occupied France, Normandy, 1944

Nog sat and brooded in a dark cellar. The shelves had once held food and wine, but now they were empty. Poverty was one of the plagues that came with war. Empty wooden crates served as furniture. A faint light came through a small, narrow window high on the wall.

Nog heard the turn of a key in the lock, and the door opened. Jake was pushed inside, and then the door slammed shut behind him. The key was turned again, and they were locked in. This might not be a holding cell in Constable Odo's office on *Deep Space Nine,* but escape was just as impossible.

"You're OK?" Nog asked.

Jake rubbed his head. That was a bad idea, since it still hurt whenever he did it, but he did it anyway. "Except for needing a new head. What about you?"

"I'd be a lot better if we could get out of here."

"Little chance of that," Jake said, sitting down on a crate. "These appear to be members of the French Resistance. They're fighting the Germans."

"Then they should help us," Nog said. His eyes brightened at the possibility of finding allies.

"I don't think so," Jake said. "They probably think we're spies. In which case, they'll execute us. Or they may believe we're innocent victims of the war. But even then, they'll keep us locked up until the war is over."

"And then we'll be executed," Nog said.

Jake looked at his friend. "Why?"

Nog went over to the wall below the window and looked up at the gray sky. "When this war is over, the Germans will have won," Nog said.

Jake started to protest. But Nog turned to Jake and put his reasoning into words.

"That has to be why the Changeling came to *this* time period. His people, the Founders, believe in order. If the Germans prevail, they will inflict order all over the planet. Freedom will have become a casualty of the war."

"And the future—our future—will be lost." As Jake spoke the words, they brought home the terrible realization of what was going to happen. "We can't let that happen, Nog."

"How can we stop it?" Nog asked. The situation seemed hopeless. The Ferengi looked around the dark room that might become their coffin. They were trapped, lost, and alone in a past that was about to be altered—and there seemed to be absolutely nothing they could do about it.

"You're Starfleet," Jake said. "Starfleet officers don't give up. Not even first-year cadets."

"I'm not giving up." Nog was adamant. "But I'm all out of ideas."

"We need to get out of here. We need to find Chief O'Brien. And stop the Changeling."

"I'll buy that," Nog said. "But, I repeat, how?"

"Well . . ." Jake looked around the room. It was as bare as his own store of ideas. Maybe their plight *was* hopeless. *Maybe . . .*

Jake was pondering their situation when he heard the turn of the key in the lock, and the door to the cellar opened. Brigitte entered, carrying a bundle of clothes in her arms. She closed the door behind her.

"You are wet and need something warm." She set the clothes down on a crate, then turned to face the wall. "Please change. I promise not to look."

While the clothes were not exactly their sizes, they were clean and warm. Jake felt a bit constricted in his outfit, and Nog's sleeves needed to be rolled up several times so he could use his hands. With an oversize cap, he looked almost human.

When they had finished dressing, Brigitte turned around and appraised the results. She barely managed to stifle a giggle. "You two look like Abbott and Costello."

"Abbott and Costello?" Jake asked. "Who are they?"

"They are American movie stars," Brigitte explained. Then she took a closer look at this odd couple and the strange clothing they had discarded. "You aren't American, are you?" she said to Jake.

Jake paused. How much could he tell this French girl? And if she did believe their story, would that knowledge damage the course of history? The alternative was to remain silent, pretend he and Nog really belonged here—which meant the Changeling would almost certainly succeed in destroying the future he came from.

He came to a decision. He had to trust someone. It might as well be Brigitte.

"OK," Jake said. "I'm going to tell you the truth."

"Jake," Nog interrupted. "We can't."

"We have to, Nog," Jake explained. "We're caught in something way beyond our control. We need help." He looked at Brigitte. "We can't do this alone. We need a friend.

"Brigitte, I'm going to tell you a story. It's a true story. I'm not sure if you're going to believe me . . . but, please, don't interrupt until I finish."

And so Jake told her everything that had happened to them during the past twenty-four hours. Nog, reluctant at first, began to fill in details whenever Jake paused. It was a very long shot, but this French girl might be their only real hope.

Jake didn't really expect Brigitte to believe him. She

would probably consider them crazy. At the worst, their tale might convince her and the others that they were spies. In which case they would be shot by their allies rather than by the enemy.

When Jake was finished, Brigitte waited a long time before responding.

"You're telling me you came from the future," she said finally. "You're chasing someone who came back . . . in *time*—to here—to make things different?"

"He's called a Changeling," Nog said. "And he has the ability to pose as anyone."

"Like a disguise?" she asked.

Jake thought that explaining Changelings and their ability to morph would be a bit too much, so he simply nodded and said, "Yes."

"We don't know why he's come here," Nog said. "But it must have something to do with the war."

Brigitte thought about this a moment. Jake could see that she hadn't totally disregarded their story. If only there were something he could tell her, something that would convince her. If only he knew why the Changeling was there and what he intended to do.

Jake let his eyes wander around the room. On one wall was a torn and faded map of France. He stepped over and looked closer at the map. *Normandy. Where's Normandy?* Suddenly it all became very clear.

"I know why the Changeling came here. I know what he intends to do." Jake turned and faced

Brigitte. "It's about the *invasion*. He's here to make certain that D day doesn't happen . . . at least not the way it did in our timeline."

"Invasion!" Brigitte said sharply. "What do you know about the invasion?"

"What's today's date?" Jake asked eagerly.

"It is the second day of June."

"In four days, the Allies will launch an invasion of Europe."

Brigitte looked at Jake. "I've heard the invasion is coming soon. But no one knows when it will be, or where."

"The invasion is called Operation Overlord. And it will happen in Normandy. Right here."

CHAPTER 8

Earth, Occupied France, Normandy, June 2, 1944

"How do you know this?" Brigitte demanded.

"Because where I came from it has already happened," Jake answered.

"What you're telling me is so difficult to believe . . . and yet, somehow, I feel you are telling me the truth."

Jake looked at the pretty French girl and wondered just what it was he had said that enabled her to believe such a fantastic story. But the important thing was that she did seem to believe him. "You'll help us?" he asked.

Brigitte hesitated. It was apparent that she was not quite ready to make the step from belief to action. But they were running out of time. "Even if you don't accept all of our story, there is another reason for you to help us."

She looked at him, and Jake continued. "The man we followed here knows about Operation Overlord and the invasion. I'm certain that he intends to reveal this to the German authorities. The invasion will fail. And, whether or not you accept that our future will change, you can be certain that your *present* will."

Brigitte understood that. "We have lived for years under the Nazi brutality . . . but always we have had hope. If the Allies fail, then so does our hope." She paused for a long moment, then made a decision. "I will help you."

"You'll tell Monsieur Jean," Jake said, hoping the French Resistance would help them.

Brigitte shook her head. "No. He would not believe your story. It would only convince him that you really are spies."

"Then—" Jake started to say.

"I will tell Uncle Maurice," Brigitte interrupted. "He will help us."

Brigitte quickly exited the cellar. Jake listened, but she did not lock the door behind her.

"It's our chance to escape," Nog said. He was also aware that the door barring their way out was no longer bolted.

Jake shook his head. "No. We must trust Brigitte."

"Even if she gets her uncle to help us, what good are a teenage girl and an old man going to be?"

Jake wondered about that, too. The four of them would be little help against even a small contingent of the German army. Still, it was better odds than they had the night before. *It'll work. It has to.*

Jake never did discover exactly what Brigitte had told Uncle Maurice. He knew it was not the story about the Changeling and the time portal. He was certain the old Frenchman would never have understood or believed such a wild tale.

But whatever she told him, Uncle Maurice was eager to help. Well, not exactly eager, but reluctantly agreeable to do his part in their plan.

It was a simple plan.

Brigitte had learned through her Resistance sources that a German colonel was taking a captured Englishman to Paris on a train later that same evening.

Jake was sure that the Englishman had to be O'Brien, and he suspected that the German colonel was actually the Changeling. Why they were going to Paris, he wasn't certain, but he knew it had to be part of the Changeling's plot to alter the outcome of the war.

They needed to rescue O'Brien and capture the Changeling. Brigitte, who had quite a knowledge of guerrilla tactics, explained how they would accomplish the task.

She pointed to a spot on the map, while explaining that it was where the train had to cross a narrow bridge spanning a river on its journey to Paris. Brigitte explained that it was the best place to make their ambush. The place was not very far from them.

The lowlands around the marshes had been flooded by the Germans as part of their defense. They now formed a lake that led into the river. They would take a boat partway, then go on foot the rest of the way to the bridge.

"What kind of ambush do you have in mind?" Nog asked.

"There are thick woods on both sides of the bridge," she explained. "If a tree should accidentally fall across the tracks, the train would have to stop on the bridge."

"We'll sneak up onto the stalled train from beneath the bridge," Nog said. "And rescue Chief O'Brien."

Jake considered the plan. It was simple and daring. They were certainly no match for the Germans in number, but the element of surprise might be enough. It had to be.

It turned out to be not quite as simple as Brigitte had laid it out on the map. There were two German soldiers patrolling the bridge, watchful for saboteurs. They had to get them to the far side of the bridge in the direction the train would be coming from in order for Uncle Maurice to plant a small explosive charge.

Uncle Maurice explained that the explosion must be just enough to topple a tree across the tracks but not powerful enough to alert the Germans. It must seem like an accident so it would not cause an alert. Surprise was their only real weapon.

TRAPPED IN TIME

Brigitte volunteered to decoy the German soldiers away from the bridge. She would pretend she had fallen and hurt herself in the hope that the soldiers would come to her aid, or at least come to investigate. But it was dangerous. If they suspected her, she would be arrested. Jake didn't like it.

"I have done this before," Brigitte told him. "It has been my role in aiding the Resistance."

Jake still didn't like it. But they had to lure the soldiers away from the bridge if their plan was to succeed.

It was late afternoon when Brigitte, Jake, and Nog set out in the boat to cross the lake to the point where it entered the river. Uncle Maurice had already left to make his way through the woods to the bridge.

When they reached the river entrance, Brigitte instructed them to pull the boat into the weeds and hide it. It would be their means of escape later that night, if all went well.

The bridge itself was not far away. They would wait until sunset, then make their way along the shore.

Jake looked at Brigitte as she stood at the edge of the lake. Seeing her silhouetted against the gray sky overhead, he wished she were someone he might have met in another time and place. For a moment, in spite of the terrible war that surrounded him, he almost wished he could remain there and get to know her better.

Beneath that youthful face and slim body was a girl who had been forced to grow up much too fast. That much they had in common, though their enemies—the Nazis and the Borg—were light-years apart.

"Do you come here a lot?" Jake asked.

"I used to. Even before the war. We were poor, and I wanted to do my part to put food on the table. So I set out snares to capture rabbits."

She stopped. From the faraway look in her eyes, Jake knew she was remembering those times, before the war.

"On the way to school," Brigitte continued, and Jake had the feeling she was sharing a special secret with him, "I would check the places where I had hidden my snares. For several weeks my snares lay empty. Then, one morning, I discovered that I had caught a beautiful rabbit by the neck in one of them."

Brigitte paused, and her eyes moistened as she recalled the event. "He was beautiful, his coat soft and silky—and he was dead. I suddenly burst into tears. Ever since then, I've never been able to take any animal's life."

Jake reached out and touched her hand. "All life is precious," he said. "There was someone who once said, 'Every man's death diminishes me.' I think I'd change *man* to *creature.*"

"I think I would, too," Brigitte said, making no attempt to break free of Jake's touch. "It's what I dread most about the invasion that will come—so many lives will be lost. So many young lives that have just begun to live."

Jake looked over at Nog and wondered if their own young lives might be among those lost if things didn't go the way they hoped.

CHAPTER 9

Earth, Occupied France, Normandy, June 2, 1944

Jake and Nog had crept along the bank on the opposite side of the river toward the bridge. It was damp and muddy, and it took them considerably longer than Jake had estimated.

But now they were cautiously clinging to the wooden underside of the bridge as they inched their way toward the center of the span. The dank smell of the creosote-soaked timbers mingled with his own sweat.

Jake was afraid. But he was also strangely eager to test his courage in a dangerous situation. It was a surreal feeling. *This must be how it is when you go to war and are about to face the enemy,* he thought.

Ahead of him, in the gloomy darkness, he could see the faint light of the locomotive coming toward them. It appeared to be the eye of some prehistoric dragon moving out of the mists of a primordial landscape.

TRAPPED IN TIME

They were knights preparing to challenge the monstrous beast.

"Only a few minutes more," Jake whispered.

"If Uncle Maurice does his part," Nog answered.

And if Brigitte does hers, Jake thought. He still didn't like the idea of her being with the German soldiers when the train stopped. They might suspect something and arrest her. But it was a chance she had been willing to take, and there was no way he could have prevented her. This was her time and her war.

Jake's foot slipped as he took a misstep. He grabbed onto a beam to steady himself. It was not much of a drop to the river below, but the noise could alert the soldiers. And it was a bit chilly for swimming, though they might well have to do just that before this night was over.

Behind them, on the far side of the bridge, there was a sharp noise, like the crack of a Jakardian sonic whip. It might have been an explosion, or it might not. The sound was muffled. If Jake had not been listening for it, he might not have heard it apart from the other night sounds. Then there was the thud of something falling, and Jake was certain.

It was the tree that Uncle Maurice had toppled. He hoped it had fallen where it was intended to fall.

They would know that soon enough. Jake felt Nog's hand on his shoulder, and he turned to see the black iron locomotive bearing down on them as it came onto the bridge.

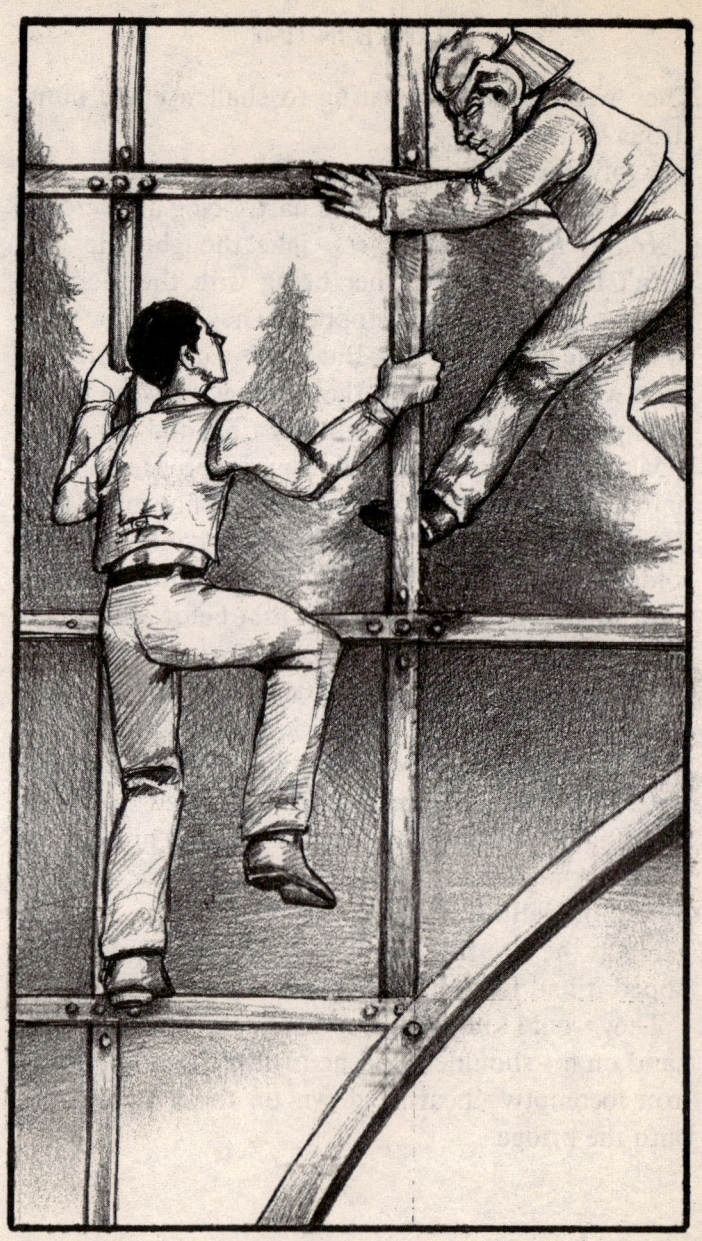

TRAPPED IN TIME

The timbers of the bridge shook as the train rumbled onto it. Jake had to steady himself to keep from tumbling off. The train did not seem to be slowing down. He began to panic. Their plan hadn't worked. The train wasn't going to stop. It would cross over the tree and continue on its route to Paris.

Then, suddenly, the massive brakes of the locomotive screeched and howled, tossing off sparks, as the train slowed and slid to a stop—right on top of them.

There were angry shouts in German. Jake heard footsteps jumping out of the train and running across the bridge away from them.

Jake waited a moment as the footsteps faded. He looked over at Nog. For better or worse, this was their moment.

"Let's do it," Nog whispered.

Together the two of them quickly climbed up onto the bridge tracks. They pressed themselves tight against the train to avoid being seen. Up ahead they saw the German soldiers who had gone to deal with the obstruction.

While pondering the next move, Jake suddenly felt a tap on his shoulder. He whirled about to see Nog. The Ferengi put his fingers to his mouth, then pointed to the second train car back from where they were.

"I'll go first," Jake whispered.

He crept toward that train car.

Jake had almost reached it when a door opened. A German soldier climbed down onto the tracks. Jake and Nog ducked under the train as the soldier passed by them.

After giving him a moment to get farther away, Jake quickly leaped up onto the steps of the car. The door to the inside of the compartment was still open. Without thinking of what was on the other side, Jake burst through.

He saw Chief O'Brien. He was tied to a chair at the far end of the compartment.

"Chief," Jake whispered loudly as he ran forward.

"Jake!" O'Brien yelled frantically. "Look out!"

Realizing that in his rush he had made a mistake, Jake turned to see a tall German colonel standing near the door. He was holding a pistol—and it was aimed at Jake.

"Good evening, young Sisko," the colonel said.

"You're—" Jake began.

"The Changeling," O'Brien finished. "He's on his way to Paris to tell the German high command all about D day."

"Chief O'Brien here can be an asset to my plan." The colonel smiled at Jake. "Unfortunately, you present more of a liability."

Jake watched in slow-motion horror as the colonel raised his pistol.

But he never finished.

Nog came through the door in a rush and hit the colonel with a pipe. The blow sent the German crashing, unconscious, to the floor.

Quickly Jake untied O'Brien, while Nog used the same ropes to bind the unconscious Changeling's hands behind his back.

"What if he wakes up?" Jake wondered, thinking that he could suddenly change into another shape—a bird or some other animal—and escape.

"That could be a problem," O'Brien admitted. He thought about it for a moment, then went to the window and tore off one of the frayed curtains.

Jake noticed that O'Brien was limping, but at least he seemed able to walk. Jake was grateful for that. One thing he and Nog hadn't anticipated was how to carry both O'Brien and the Changeling from the bridge to the boat.

"Blindfold him," O'Brien said. "He won't know where he is, and that will at least slow him down."

While Jake tied the curtain around the colonel's eyes, O'Brien reached inside the German's coat. He found what he was looking for: the time portal device.

"This is our ticket home," O'Brien said as he looked at the device.

"We should use it now," Nog said. "Return to the future, with the Changeling."

"Good idea," O'Brien replied. But as he studied the device, he began to frown. "Unfortunately, it's going to take me some time to figure out how this gadget works." He looked at the unconscious Changeling. "And I don't favor the odds of him telling us how it operates."

TRAPPED IN TIME

Outside there were footsteps and voices, and they were coming toward them.

"Time we were going, lads." O'Brien tossed the device to Jake. "Take care of that. Or we'll end up dying here of old age before we're ever born."

Jake put the device inside his jacket. Nog helped O'Brien carry the colonel to the door of the train car.

German soldiers were returning from the far end of the bridge. From the sound of their voices, they had removed the blockade. They were also not in much of a hurry, so apparently they did not suspect sabotage.

With as much stealth as possible when dragging something large and heavy, O'Brien and Nog carried the dead weight of the Changeling colonel along the tracks, keeping the train between them and the soldiers. Their plan was to pull him under the train and to slip down off the bridge near the riverbank. Then they could use the thick weeds to hide their escape.

But the best-laid plans do not always go as expected.

Jake was so intent on watching O'Brien and Nog's progress that he failed to notice one of the German bridge guards approaching.

"Halt!" The command was loud and in German, but there was no mistaking the intent.

Jake was too far away to do anything. The guard raised his rifle. Jake wasn't sure if he had orders to shoot first and ask questions later, but that appeared likely.

Now, from the opposite end of the bridge, he heard the shouts and running feet of the other German soldiers. They were about to be surrounded.

"Halt!" The German guard shouted the command again. This time Jake had no doubts about whether or not he would shoot O'Brien and Nog.

Then, out of nowhere, Brigitte came running headfirst into the guard, knocking him off balance so that his shot went wild.

"Go!" Brigitte shouted.

O'Brien and Nog did not hesitate. They pushed the unconscious Changeling down the bank at the edge of the bridge. And leaped after him.

Where he was, between the train cars, Jake had not yet been seen. He had a moment of surprise. Seeing Brigitte struggling with the German guard, he knew he had to help her.

But before he could move, Brigitte broke free of the guard and started to run.

For a moment, Jake watched as she ran along the tracks. Then, as if he were trapped in a slow-motion holosuite drama, he watched as the guard retrieved his rifle, raised, aimed—and fired.

It was as if the bullet had struck him as Jake saw Brigitte freeze in place from the impact. Then, slowly, she stumbled another step to the edge of the bridge.

Horrified, Jake saw Brigitte fall over the edge, plummeting into the dark waters of the river.

CHAPTER 10

Earth, Occupied France, Normandy, June 2, 1944

Jake came out of his hiding place like a shot. He dived off the bridge into the dark waters.

He swam toward the spot where Brigitte had plunged into the river. Around him he could hear shouts and sharp echoes of bullets being fired. But he was oblivious to everything but the single task of reaching Brigitte.

He was a good swimmer and crossed the distance to where she should be in good time. But she wasn't there. She hadn't emerged from the murky void.

Jake dived beneath the surface.

The night and the dark swirling waters made it impossible for him to see. He was becoming frantic. *How long has it been? She'll drown if I don't find her soon.*

TRAPPED IN TIME

He reached out frantically. He had dived without taking a breath. His lungs were almost bursting. But he wasn't going to give up.

Suddenly, he felt something. It was a leg. No, it was an arm. It was Brigitte's arm.

Jake reached out, grabbed the arm. Now his lungs were bursting. Slowly, or so it seemed, he pulled Brigitte toward the surface.

Why is it so far away? The river shouldn't be this deep. For a tense moment, Jake was confused. In the darkness of night there was no bright sunlight to lead the way.

Then, with a final gasp, he broke through the surface with Brigitte. He swallowed the air in deep, urgent gulps. It tasted wonderful.

Brigitte? He looked at the slim, unconscious girl in his arms. *Is she breathing?* He couldn't be certain. He had to reach the shore. *But which way is it?*

Suddenly, he was not alone. Chief O'Brien had swum up beside him. Without a word, O'Brien took Brigitte's other arm and started off. Jake followed alongside, trusting that the chief knew where he was going.

The riverbank was closer than Jake had thought. O'Brien pulled Brigitte up onto the damp weeds. Jake immediately bent over her and began mouth-to-mouth resuscitation.

There was a long, terrible moment. Then Brigitte stirred. She spit up water, coughed, and began breathing. She looked up at Jake and smiled faintly. It was the most wonderful smile he had ever seen.

"I thought you were shot," Jake said. He looked for a wound but could find none.

"So did I," Brigitte said. "But the soldier missed, or he was firing a warning shot. I tripped and fell."

"We can discuss this later," O'Brien whispered, with a pat on Jake's shoulder. "Right now we'd better be gettin' away from here."

In the frantic chaos of the last few minutes, Jake had almost forgotten where they were. Now the sharp sounds of rifle fire from the bridge brought him back to reality.

"They're shooting at us," Jake said.

"No," O'Brien said as he looked across the river toward the bridge. "It's the French Resistance. They're shooting at the Germans." He looked at Brigitte. "Seems they must have heard about our troubles, and came to help."

"Uncle Maurice," Brigitte said. "He must have told Monsieur Jean."

O'Brien looked confused at the mention of the unfamiliar names. "I'll explain later," Jake said. "Right now, we'd better follow your advice and get out of here."

They moved through the weeds toward the place where Nog was guarding the unconscious Changeling. O'Brien led the way. Jake followed, helping Brigitte, who was still exhausted from her ordeal.

"I'm sorry," Brigitte said when she stumbled and nearly caused Jake to fall.

"It's OK," he replied. And it was. He didn't mind having her this close to him. He only wished the circumstances could have been more pleasant.

Up ahead O'Brien had stopped. "Nog should be here," he said.

But as Jake approached, he saw that the Ferengi wasn't in the small clearing in the marsh. And neither was the Changeling.

"Maybe he went on ahead to the boat," Brigitte suggested.

"Not dragging the Changeling with him," O'Brien said.

"The Resistance might have come along and helped," Jake said. He didn't believe that, but he would have liked to. The alternatives weren't pleasant to comprehend.

"Where's your boat?" O'Brien asked.

"About three hundred meters down that way," Jake said, pointing.

"Then you and the young lady head for it," O'Brien said in a voice used to giving commands. "I'll search for Nog and meet you there."

"But—" Jake started to complain. Nog was his best friend. He wasn't about to leave him.

"I know how you feel," O'Brien said. "But you've got her to look after. I'll find Nog. I promise."

Jake didn't like it, but the chief's logic was correct. One of them had to stay with Brigitte and get her to safety.

So, while O'Brien remained behind, Jake and Brigitte moved through the marshy ground toward the boat.

They had hidden the boat in a dense patch of weeds. There were trees between it and the bridge so that they wouldn't be seen by German patrols who frequented the area.

It was wet and cold moving through the marsh. Jake kept them closer to the river, rather than moving inland where the ground would be firmer but they would have been more likely to encounter a German patrol. With all the action at the bridge, Jake was certain that there would be Germans all over the area very soon.

What he didn't expect was to run into them this soon. Moving as quietly as possible through the darkness, Jake and Brigitte stopped short as a broad-shouldered man stepped out of nowhere, blocking their path.

From the distance, through the wet mist, Jake couldn't see who the man was. But he could see the rifle the man carried in a ready position.

Then, from another angle, a second man appeared. Followed by a third. They all carried weapons.

What do I do now? Jake wondered to himself.

Brigitte squeezed his hand. Had he rescued her from the river, only to deliver her into a German prison?

"Bon soir." The voice that came from behind them was familiar.

TRAPPED IN TIME

Slowly, still holding Brigitte's hand, Jake turned and found himself facing Monsieur Jean.

The tall Frenchman smiled politely. "Rather late to be out for a walk, isn't it?"

"We were, ah—" Jake stammered.

"I *know* what you were trying to do." Monsieur Jean looked at Brigitte. "Uncle Maurice told me. He thought you might get into trouble."

In the distance Jake heard another round of shooting from the direction of the bridge. Monsieur Jean looked over his shoulder. "My men will lead the Germans off in the wrong direction. But the Germans are not stupid. We need to leave here . . . quickly. Robert, give us a hand."

One of the Resistance fighters stepped over and helped Brigitte. Monsieur Jean walked beside Jake as they moved through the marsh.

"Your attempt to rescue your friend was ill advised," Monsieur Jean said. Then he clasped a big hand on Jake's shoulder. "But I admire your bravery."

Suddenly, Jake became aware that they were not heading toward the boat. He stopped.

"Not to worry," Monsieur Jean said. "The boat will be retrieved later . . . when things are quieter."

It was not the boat that Jake was worrying about, but O'Brien and Nog. "I have to wait for my friends."

"The Irishman and the strange one with the big ears are safe," Monsieur Jean said. "I promise."

That eased Jake's mind—until he realized that

Monsieur Jean had not mentioned the real reason they were here, in this time period. The Changeling.

"The German colonel?" Jake asked.

"Escaped, I'm afraid. But not to worry. We will find him."

But will we find him in time? Jake thought. *Will we find him in time?*

CHAPTER 11

Earth, Occupied France, Normandy, June 3, 1944

As Monsieur Jean had promised, O'Brien and Nog arrived at the cottage shortly after Jake, Brigitte, and the French Resistance fighters. Uncle Maurice had found Nog in the marshes. The Changeling had morphed and escaped. He could now be anyone—or anything.

"I feel stupid," Nog said.

"Not your fault." Jake tried to reassure his friend. "We should have known the blindfold was not enough. We needed a stasis field."

"Unfortunately, lads, the closest one is several hundred years in the future." O'Brien pondered the situation as he sat with Jake and Nog in a corner of the room.

"We'll have to figure out another way to contain him," Nog said. "The next time we meet."

"What if there isn't a next time?" Jake contemplated the worst-case scenario.

"There will be," Nog replied. He pointed at Jake's jacket. "You have his only ticket home."

"If he intends to go home." O'Brien said.

They both looked at the chief, who continued. "The Changeling may not be planning on returning to the future. While I hate to admit it, it's quite likely that we may never see him again."

If that's true, Jake thought, *then we've failed.* They still had the means to return to the future, but if it was the future of the Changeling, would they want to go back?

As morning approached, the atmosphere inside the cottage was as thick as the fog outside. It had been a long, sleepless night for everyone.

While Monsieur Jean and the others in the French Resistance appeared to accept Jake, Nog, and O'Brien as allies, they still had many unanswered questions.

Fortunately, O'Brien, who had played a hundred Battle of Britain simulations with Dr. Bashir in Quark's holosuites, knew enough World War II history to come up with what he hoped was a convincing story. They were helping the Allied forces, scouting ahead to make sure the invasion happened as planned. The colonel was a traitor who had to be stopped before he alerted the German command in Paris. *Not a bad story,* Jake thought. *And not too far from the truth.*

TRAPPED IN TIME

But Jake was anxious. Not so much about whether or not the Resistance accepted him—though that did concern him—but about the fact that the Changeling had escaped and they had no idea how to find him.

"He'll try to go to Paris," Nog suggested, sitting on the floor in a corner with Jake. Across the room, O'Brien sat at the table under the bare lightbulb with Monsieur Jean and Uncle Maurice. The man called Robert had led the other Resistance members out to search for Colonel Kruger. But Jake was certain that the Changeling had taken another form by now. He could be anyone—and anywhere.

Overhead the bare bulb hung down from the ceiling, casting shadows. To Jake it made the whole scene seem unreal. It reminded him of a holosuite game, except that here the computer wouldn't freeze the program if things got sticky.

Brigitte entered the room, carrying a wooden tray that contained five cups of coffee. After setting three down on the table, she brought the remaining two over to Jake and Nog.

Jake took a sip of the brown liquid. It was hot but definitely not up to replicator standards. His grandfather would not serve this weak brew in his New Orleans restaurant.

"Sorry," Brigitte said, noticing Jake's tepid response to the coffee. "With the war, our supplies are low. I have to stretch the coffee beans."

"No." Jake apologized for his apparent reaction. "It's fine."

Brigitte slid down and sat on the floor next to him. "No. It's not."

"Hey, I like it." Nog smiled and swallowed. Jake wondered if he'd picked up a few of the local grubs to add flavor to the brew.

"You were saying," Jake said to Nog, turning the conversation from coffee back to the Changeling.

"Paris, is what I was saying," Nog replied. "That's where he was headed. And that's where he'll be going."

"Why Paris?" Jake asked.

"It's close enough," Nog said. "The German command is there. And he doesn't have time to go all the way to Berlin."

"But will they believe him?" Brigitte asked.

"I don't think that matters," Jake said. Nog and Brigitte looked at him, wondering what he meant. Jake took an obligatory sip of the coffee and explained. "He can become whoever he chooses. Rather than convince a general to believe his story, he can *become* the general and give the orders to prepare for the Allied invasion."

"We must tell the Allies," Brigitte insisted. "They must change the invasion plans!"

"No!" Jake almost shouted. They couldn't start changing history to avoid . . . changing history. It was giving Jake a headache sorting out the logic of time.

"Besides, why would they believe us? Even if we gave them details of the invasion, they'd only think we were spies."

"We must do something," Brigitte said with passion. Whatever she believed about their time travel tale, it was obvious she did accept that the coming invasion was in jeopardy. And if it failed, the war might be lost to the enemy. That was the very real, *present* danger.

Jake understood that, and he was as impatient as she to do something. *But what?* He looked across the room at O'Brien sitting with the two Frenchmen. Even if Monsieur Jean actually believed their story, he and his Resistance movement would not be able to help them.

Jake touched the time portal device in his pocket. O'Brien had figured out how to use it to get them back to the future. They didn't need Vance's retinal scan. The professor had programmed in a return loop. When the portal was activated again they should return to the lab in twenty-fourth-century France. *Should* . . . Their only real hope now was that the Changeling would need to return to the future—if only to determine if he had succeeded—and when he did, they could catch him. *It is a real long shot,* Jake thought. But it might be the only shot they had.

"I have to make breakfast," Brigitte said, which caused Jake to realize they hadn't eaten in a while. He was hungry. "Would you like to help?"

It was an invitation Jake couldn't refuse. He followed Brigitte into the kitchen.

Not that it was much of a kitchen. It was almost as bare as the rest of the cottage. There was a small wood-burning stove, a table that alternated between being a place for preparing a meal and a place for eating it, and what looked like an old-fashioned radio on a shelf above the table.

Life in the twentieth century was pretty primitive, Jake thought. Still, looking at Brigitte, he was sure he could get to like it—if there wasn't a war on.

From the other room he heard the sound of the door opening and someone entering. Probably one of the Resistance men reporting in.

But when he looked through the doorway, he saw Nog, O'Brien, Monsieur Jean, and Uncle Maurice staring at the man who had entered, as if they had seen a ghost. And in the case of Monsieur Jean, it seemed that he had. For the man who entered was Monsieur Jean, and he cradled a rifle in his arms.

"Please not to move," the man said. He looked over at Monsieur Jean, who sat next to O'Brien at the table. "That man is . . . an impostor."

Jake slid back from the kitchen doorway, hoping the man had not seen him. Either he or the Monsieur Jean sitting at the table was the Changeling.

But the question was, *which one?*

Brigitte was about to speak, but Jake motioned for her to be silent. They stepped farther back into the kitchen, while Jake tried to figure out what to do.

He had two problems. The first one was to determine who was real and who was the Changeling. But even

if he knew which one it was, he still had to find a way to immobilize the alien before he could morph and escape.

A blood sample would prove who was human and who was not. Changeling blood did not coagulate and, in fact, showed all the properties of the Changeling. But Jake doubted that either of the Monsieur Jeans would allow that test to happen.

No. He had to reason this out. Then make his move based on that decision.

But which one is the Changeling?

The one who just came in was certainly the aggressor. But, on the other hand, he might be the real Monsieur Jean, carrying a weapon because he couldn't be sure what was going on. Jake gave equal weight to both possibilities.

Jake had to get one of them to reveal himself. Then he had to figure out how to contain someone who could instantly dissolve into a formless shape and escape.

He looked around the kitchen. An idea struck him. It might work. It had to. He whispered some quick instructions to Brigitte, then entered the other room.

"Hold it," the Monsieur Jean with the rifle said as he saw Jake.

Jake froze. If only he could be sure who was real and who was a duplicate. He looked at both Frenchmen. There was no way to tell for sure. Their looks, their voices, even their mannerisms were identical.

"He's after the device," O'Brien said. "That's why he's here."

"Yes," the Monsieur Jean at the table said. Suddenly he morphed out a tentacle-like arm and grabbed the weapon from the startled Monsieur Jean at the door.

"This weapon is an antique but sufficient to inflict damage." The arm of the Monsieur Jean at the table morphed back into human form. He stood up with the rifle. He looked at Jake. "I do want my device back. Once I've informed the German high command of the Allies' D day plans, I must return to be certain that history has been altered."

TRAPPED IN TIME

"It's in the kitchen," Jake said. "I was working on it."

The Changeling stepped forward and looked through the kitchen door, all the while keeping an eye on the men in the other room. The device was, as Jake had said, lying on the table. Brigitte was nowhere to be seen.

Jake had been afraid that the Changeling would order him to retrieve the device, but that didn't happen. The Changeling came into the kitchen and moved toward the table. As soon as he had the device, he would morph and make his escape. And it would be impossible to stop him.

Except that, as Jake had hoped, in his haste the Changeling was concentrating on the device on the table and not noticing the wet floor where Brigitte had just poured a bucket of water. Nor did he see the bare wires torn from the portable generator used to power the shortwave radio used by the Resistance. Not until he stepped on the wire.

"Now!" Jake shouted.

From her vantage point inside the walk-in cupboard, Brigitte hit the generator's power switch. There was a sudden arc of electricity that sprang from the wires on the wet floor and ran up the body of the Changeling.

Quickly Jake grabbed another bucket and splashed water on the Changeling, increasing the voltage that surged up through his alien body and preventing him from morphing.

O'Brien was now in the kitchen. He picked up a rolling pin and slammed the Changeling hard, knocking him unconscious.

"You can shut it down now," O'Brien said, and they watched as the electrical arcing stopped.

"Is he . . . ?" Jake asked as O'Brien leaned down to examine the Changeling.

"He'll survive," O'Brien said. Then the chief engineer stepped over to the table and retrieved the time portal device.

Nog, Monsieur Jean, and Uncle Maurice entered the kitchen. The two Frenchmen were confused.

"Just what is going on?" Monsieur Jean demanded.

"We have to get this man back to Allied headquarters," O'Brien explained in his most official voice. "There is a rendezvous point. But I'll need a vehicle. Can you and Uncle Maurice get us one?"

Monsieur Jean nodded. "We'll be right back." The two Frenchmen left.

O'Brien looked at Jake and Nog. "I wanted them out of the way while I open the time portal." He looked at Brigitte. "You seem to know a lot of what's been going on. I'll leave it to you to make up a story about where we've gone."

"I'll do that," Brigitte said. "But the invasion? Is it really going to happen here?"

"Yes," O'Brien said. "That much I can tell you."

"And," Nog added, "you do win."

O'Brien activated the time device. There was a single instant when Jake wasn't sure it was going to work. Then there was a pulsating cube of incredible light forming a vortex in the center of the room.

Rapidly the vortex grew and became a rectangle large enough to enter. It was their doorway home.

"Let's go, lads," O'Brien said. He had hold of the Changeling and pulled him as he entered the vortex of the portal—and vanished. Then Nog followed, and he, too, was gone.

Brigitte looked at the sight with eyes filled with amazement. "Now I believe you, Jake," she said.

Jake stepped forward and prepared to follow his friends through the portal, but Brigitte touched his hand, and he hesitated.

"I have to go," Jake said. Already the portal was beginning to shrink.

"I know," Brigitte said. "There is something I want to give you. I know there is no time. Only tell me the date where you are going."

Jake told her. Quickly she leaned forward and kissed him. "Do not forget me, Jake Sisko."

"I won't," Jake promised. There was a moment of indecision, when he wondered if it might not be possible to stay. He had a brief, terrible thought that Brigitte might die in the war.

"You must go now," Brigitte said urgently.

Jake turned and saw the portal wavering as it continued to shrink. In a few more seconds he wouldn't be able to get through. He had to go *now*.

With one final look back, Jake stepped up and entered the vortex . . . and as he was swallowed by the abyss, he fell forward into the future.

CHAPTER 12

Earth, Paris, 24th Century

In a single instant, Jake stepped from the middle of the twentieth century back into the twenty-fourth.

One moment he was with Brigitte in the cottage on the Normandy coast, and the next was in Professor Vance's laboratory in Paris.

Behind him the time portal closed. The link between the generations was broken.

Jake saw that Nog and O'Brien had hold of the Changeling, who still appeared to be Monsieur Jean. The professor and his assistant, Pierre, were anxiously watching, not quite certain what was going on.

"I'll contact Starfleet security," O'Brien was saying. He looked at Nog. "Make sure he stays unconscious until they arrive. If you can't find a phaser to stun him with, then hit him over the head."

"I have a better idea," Professor Vance offered. "Put the Changeling on the table."

Nog and O'Brien complied, dragging the Changeling and lifting him onto the table.

"Now step back," the professor said.

They did. "Computer. Activate stasis field," Professor Vance said aloud.

"Stasis field activated," came the familiar female computer voice. *Do all Federation computers speak with the same voice?* Jake wondered. Probably so. Or, at least, every computer he had ever heard.

O'Brien left the room with Pierre to notify Starfleet. Jake and Nog remained with Professor Vance. The professor was doing something in a corner of the room, while Jake kept an eye on the Changeling. He saw that he was waking up.

The Changeling looked around the room. He touched the edge of the stasis field, and a mild jolt shocked him back to the table.

The Changeling began to shimmer and dissolve into a golden gelatinous state. Jake had seen Constable Odo do the same thing on *Deep Space Nine*. *How exciting it must be to become anything or anyone you want,* he had thought. *But then,* he began to wonder, *if you could do that—would you ever know who you really were?*

Nog stepped toward the stasis field. "He's going to escape."

"Don't worry," Professor Vance said as he joined

them. "Not even an atom can pass through this stasis field."

And, Jake saw, the professor was right. After trying to dissolve through the field, the Changeling gave up and returned to the humanoid state of Monsieur Jean.

Professor Vance stepped over to the edge of the stasis field. He had the time portal device in his hand. He showed it to the Changeling. "You tried to use my invention to change the history of my world."

"But he failed," Jake said.

"Yes. But others will try, and they may succeed." The professor looked at the device in his hand. "Temporal anomalies happen. But to be able to travel the time stream at will is something still too dangerous to allow into the wrong hands."

"Starfleet will take care of your invention," Nog said.

"Perhaps. But even in the hallowed halls of Starfleet are those who might misuse such power."

"But," Jake interrupted, "you've invented the device. How can you un-invent it?"

"Like this," Professor Vance said. He activated the time device, and a portal began to open.

"Professor!" O'Brien shouted as he entered the room, accompanied by two Starfleet security guards. "What're you doing?"

"Sending this where it won't do any more harm—five million years back into Earth's past."

Before O'Brien could stop him, the professor

hurled the time device through the portal. It vanished.

O'Brien rushed toward the portal, but Jake stopped him. "I don't think you want to go through there."

O'Brien hesitated. "You're right, Jake. Five million years ago isn't a good place to visit."

Then the portal closed—*forever*.

Two days later Jake and Nog walked through the grassy plaza of Starfleet Academy. The early fog had burned off the bay, and it was turning into another bright San Francisco morning.

"Starfleet is not happy with Professor Vance for shutting down his experiment," Nog said.

"Time travel is still going to be with us," Jake replied. "In spite of what Professor Vance did. There have already been several temporal disturbances in this decade. Enough to cause the Federation to create a Department of Temporal Investigations."

"Which reminds me," Nog said. "I have an appointment with them in an hour."

"I've been told to expect a visit from them after I return to *Deep Space Nine*," Jake said.

They had walked to a green bluff overlooking the Academy and the bay beyond. Sailboats rode the waves, while hovercraft floated overhead. Jake always liked this city and enjoyed visits here with his parents when he was growing up. In some ways he was almost jealous of Nog's Academy experience here.

But Starfleet was not for him. Even his father knew that and no longer prodded Jake.

"Time to go," Jake said reluctantly. "Chief O'Brien is finished with the modifications to the *Defiant,* and we're headed back to *Deep Space Nine.*"

"I'm going to miss you, Jake," Nog said. He seemed on the verge of getting sentimental—and Ferengi never get sentimental.

"I'll miss you, too, Nog."

"Hey. It's not forever," Nog said. "My sophomore year starts in a few months. I'll have a field assignment. Maybe it will be on *Deep Space Nine.*"

"That would be great," Jake said.

They shook hands, and then, in a kind of awkward moment, they hugged. Nog turned and walked away toward the towering spires of Starfleet Academy. Even if Nog did come to *Deep Space Nine* for a duty tour, it would never be quite the same as it was. *I guess that's the hard part of growing up,* Jake thought.

Jake hurried to meet O'Brien at the transporter station. Earth was nice, but it was good to be going home to *Deep Space Nine.*

But when Jake arrived, he was informed that their immediate destination was not the *Defiant.* "A slight detour," O'Brien said as he ushered Jake onto the transporter platform. "A friend of mine has asked to meet you."

Before Jake could ask who the friend was, they were

enveloped in the beam and had arrived in the transporter room of a starship.

It could have been any Starfleet ship, but when Jake saw the man in the commander's uniform who was waiting for them, he knew instantly where he was even before the man spoke.

"Welcome to the *Enterprise*," invited Captain Jean-Luc Picard.

CHAPTER 13

Earth, France, 24th Century

Jake had seen the *U.S.S. Enterprise* once before. It was the starship that had brought the first runabouts to *Deep Space Nine*. But, he remembered, that *Enterprise*, the *NCC-1701D*, had been destroyed. This was the new *Enterprise-E*. But Jean-Luc Picard was still her captain.

"If you don't mind, Jake . . . may I call you Jake?"

Jake nodded. Captain Picard stepped forward onto the transporter platform. As if it been previously choreographed, O'Brien stepped off the platform. "We could go to my quarters," Picard said. "But I have another place in mind for our meeting."

Picard raised his hand, and the transporter officer keyed in the coordinates. Jake and Picard beamed off the *Enterprise* to . . .

"This is Provence," Picard said as they materialized in late afternoon in a sunny vineyard on a gentle slope in the rural French countryside.

Jake breathed in the sweet summer air. This was France, but it was far removed from the chilly marshes of Normandy.

"That is my home." Captain Picard pointed to a white house in the valley that surrounded the vineyards. It was not fancy, but it seemed like a castle compared to the little cottage where Brigitte had lived. Suddenly Jake wondered if that cottage was still there, then thought that the notion was silly. Even if it had somehow managed to survive the war, there was no way it could have withstood the onslaught of the centuries between then and now.

"Or it *was* my home," Picard corrected as he started down the hill. "Until I left to wander the stars."

Halfway down the hillside, Picard paused. He reached down and pulled a single grape from a vine, staring at it as if it were pure latinum. "But my roots will always be here, just like these vines. I was born here, and, God willing, this is where I'll come to die."

They continued the rest of the way to the house in silence. Jake enjoyed the warm day and pleasant surrounds, but he wondered why Captain Picard had brought him here.

Entering the house, Picard explained that his sister-in-law was away, which accounted for the house being empty. Picard went straight into the library, and Jake followed.

TRAPPED IN TIME

It was, Jake observed, a well-used library. The books on the shelves showed wear. Not the wear of neglect but that of having been read and reread many times. Many of the books were old, some very old. There was a history here that told of a land and a family.

"Our family history has always been important to the Picards. When my brother and his son died in a fire last year . . ." Picard's voice broke momentarily as he recalled the terrible event. "It was in the winery. Somehow a blaze started. Robert and Rene tried to put it out. My brother was so old-fashioned . . . he hated technology. Robert never installed a suppression system. They were trapped . . . burned to death."

"I'm sorry." It was all Jake could say.

"My brother and I never got along. He was the traditionalist. Continuing the Picard family line was so important to him." Picard looked at Jake. "You know there was a Picard who fought at Trafalgar . . . and Picards who settled the first Martian colony. When Robert married and had a son, well, I no longer felt a need to carry on the family line." Picard paused, looked around the room. "Now the responsibility has fallen upon my shoulders to continue our line. It is a burden I did not wish."

Picard stepped over and removed one particular book from the shelf. He handed it to Jake.

The book was Victor Hugo's novel of the French Revolution, *Les Misérables*. It was a rather plain-

looking book and was extremely old. But special care had been taken to preserve it from the ravages of time.

"My ancestor settled here in the middle of the twentieth century. From that point on, this place became the Picard home. We've been here for centuries."

Jake held the book, not quite sure what to do with it or what to say. Picard stepped over to the wall where

TRAPPED IN TIME

there was a group of pictures. Even at a distance, Jake could tell that it was a kind of family collage.

"This was Robert Picard," Picard said as he pointed to a photograph of a young man and woman. "He was the one who came here first. My brother is named for him."

Jake looked at the picture, not at the man but at the woman. The photograph was faded and slightly out of focus, but still he recognized her instantly. "Brigitte."

"Brigitte Picard. She married Robert shortly after Earth's Second World War, and they moved here."

Now Jake opened the book. He saw an inscription on the title page: *To Jake, for giving us all a future. Love always and forever, Brigitte.*

Jake's eyes moistened, and the words blurred. Captain Picard's voice suddenly seemed distant. "She wrote you a note. It's been passed down from generation to generation—until now."

Picard opened a desk drawer, took out a small envelope, and handed it to Jake. It was sealed. "Read it later. On your way back on the *Defiant*."

"You don't want to know what it says?" Jake asked as he slid the envelope into the book.

"The words in there belong to you. I, and my family, are only the messengers. This was inside another envelope. It had yesterday's date on it. No one in the family had any idea what it meant, but we waited, until now. The instructions inside are the reason I had Chief O'Brien beam you to the *Enterprise*."

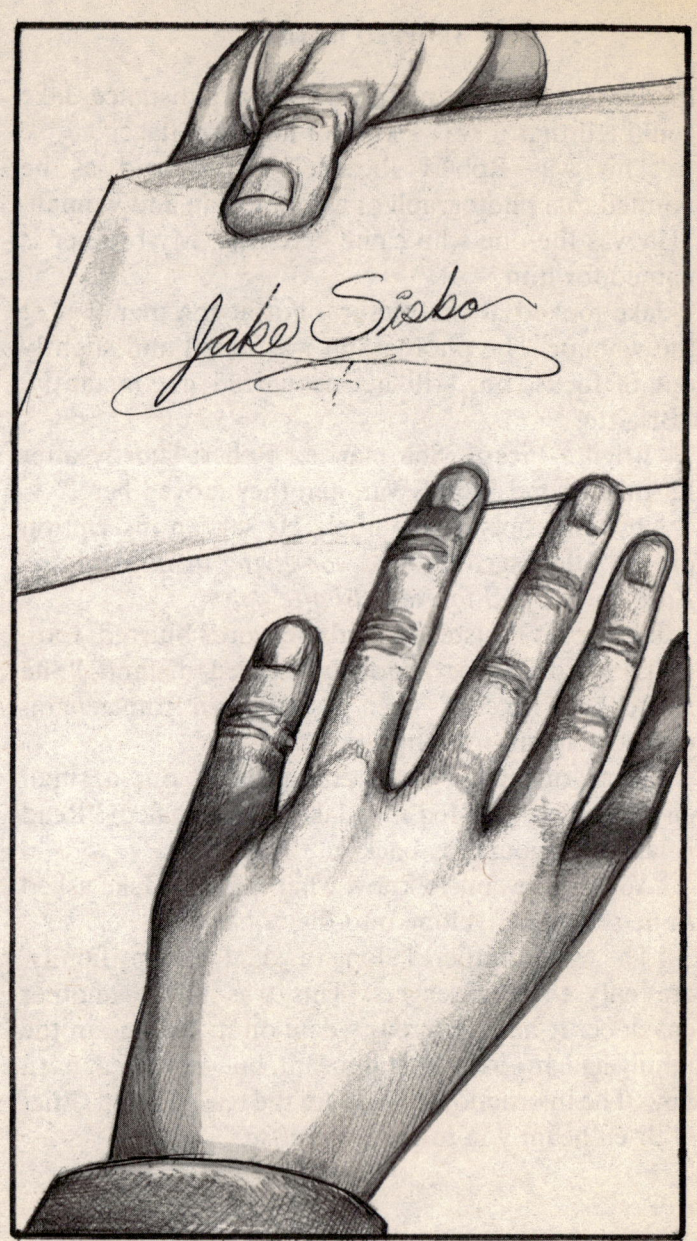

TRAPPED IN TIME

Jake opened his mouth, but there were no words. He knew he should say something but didn't know what to say. Picard raised his hand, as if understanding Jake's predicament. "Don't say anything now. Later, if you like, we can talk."

"Thank you," was what Jake finally said.

"No, Mister Sisko. It's you I have to thank. You may have helped to save the future from tyranny, but in a way, that seems almost unimportant. You saved the life of a young French girl four centuries ago—and thereby saved the lives of my family and myself."

EPILOGUE

**Deep Space Nine, Alpha Quadrant,
Three Weeks Later**

"That's quite a story," Dulmur said when Jake had finished.

"Indeed," Lusly commented.

"It's everything as I remember," Jake said. *Well, not exactly everything,* he thought. He had left off the part about Captain Picard and the letter from Brigitte. He didn't think it was important to the course of history, and, besides, it really wasn't any of their business.

Dulmur looked at Lusly. "I think we have everything."

"Indeed," Lusly replied.

Dulmur looked at Jake. "Thank you for your time, Mister Sisko."

"We will enter your statement into the temporal archives," Lusly added.

* * *

Afterward, when the two Temporal policemen had left *Deep Space Nine,* Jake went to his favorite perch above the Promenade, where he and Nog used to sit for hours observing the ever-changing flow of humans and aliens below. And through the huge windows on the other side of the Promenade, they could watch the ships leaving the station, bound for distant starports in the Gamma Quadrant on the other side of the Bajoran wormhole.

This was the place they came to dream about what was to be. And it was here that Jake now came to think and to write.

And to read. He took the note from Brigitte out of his pocket. He had already read it several times, but here, in this place, it seemed appropriate to read it again.

Dearest Jake,
When, and if, you read this, centuries will have passed between my world and yours. The terrible war is now over. My only hope, as we move forward into our future, is that such an evil thing will never happen again. But whatever fate befalls me, I will always remember you.
All my love and affection,
Brigitte

Jake folded the note neatly and tucked it back into his pocket. He knew, from what Captain Picard had told him, that Brigitte's fate had been a good one.

Now he raised his eyes to look out at the vast starscape spreading beyond the space station, and he looked forward with anticipation to his own future.

About the Author

TED PEDERSEN began his career writing programs for computers in Seattle before making the long trek south to Los Angeles to write for TV. He has authored more than one hundred episodes for such landmark animation series as *Teenage Mutant Ninja Turtles, Exosquad, X-Men,* and *Mummies.* More recently he started writing books, and these include *Internet for Kids, The Tale of the Virtual Nightmare* in the *Are You Afraid of the Dark?* series, and three previous *Deep Space Nine* YA novels, *The Pet, Gypsy World,* and *Space Camp.* He is currently working on his next contribution to the series. When not out wandering the World Wide Web, Ted hangs out in Venice, California, with his wife, Phyllis, and their menagerie of cats and computers.

About the Illustrator

TODD CAMERON HAMILTON is a self-taught artist who has resided all his life in Chicago, Illinois. He has been a professional illustrator for the past ten years, specializing in fantasy, science fiction, and horror. Todd is the current president of the Association of Science Fiction and Fantasy Artists. His original works grace many private and corporate collections. He has coauthored two novels and several short stories. When he is not drawing, painting, or writing, his interests include metalsmithing, puppetry, and teaching.

Join the STAR TREK™ Fan Club

For only $19.95 you can join **Paramount Pictures' Official** *Star Trek* **Fan Club!** Membership to this exclusive organization includes:

- **A one-year subscription** to the bimonthly *Star Trek Communicator* magazine packed with *Star Trek* photos, interviews and articles! Plus a merchandise insert filled with the latest and greatest *Star Trek* collectibles.
- **Membership kit** which includes an exclusive set of **Skybox Trading Cards, exclusive collectors' poster, and more!**
- **Discounts** on *Star Trek* merchandise!
- **Opportunity** to purchase exclusive *Star Trek* **collectibles** available to members only!

Yes! I want to join The Official *Star Trek* Fan Club!
Membership for one-year - $19.95 (Canadian $22.95-U.S. Dollars)
☐ To join by VISA/MasterCard only call **1-800-TRUE-FAN (1-800-878-3326)**
☐ I've enclosed my check or money order for $19.95

Name _____
Address _____
City/State _____ Zip _____
Send to:
The Official *Star Trek* Fan Club, P.O. Box 55841, Boulder, CO 80322-5841

TM, ® & © 1996 Paramount Pictures. All Rights Reserved.

1251

Pocket Books presents a new, illustrated series for younger readers based on the hit television show:

STAR TREK: DEEP SPACE NINE®

Young Jake Sisko is looking for friends aboard the space station. He finds Nog, a Ferengi his own age, and together they find a whole lot of trouble!

#1: THE STAR GHOST

#2: STOWAWAYS
by Brad Strickland

#3: PRISONERS OF PEACE
by John Peel

#4: THE PET
by Mel Gilden and Ted Pedersen

#5: ARCADE
by Diana G. Gallagher

#6: FIELD TRIP
by John Peel

#7: GYPSY WORLD
by Ted Pedersen

#8: HIGHEST SCORE
by Kem Antilles

#9: CARDASSIAN IMPS
by Mel Gilden

#10: SPACE CAMP
by Ted Pedersen

#11: DAY OF HONOR: HONOR BOUND
by Diana G. Gallagher

#12: TRAPPED IN TIME
by Ted Pedersen

TM, ® & © 1997 Paramount Pictures. All Rights Reserved.

Published by Pocket Books

BLAST OFF ON NEW ADVENTURES FOR THE YOUNGER READER!

Before they became officers aboard the U.S.S. Enterprise™, your favorite characters struggled through the Academy....

STAR TREK
THE NEXT GENERATION®
STARFLEET ACADEMY®

#1: WORF'S FIRST ADVENTURE
#2: LINE OF FIRE
#3: SURVIVAL
by Peter David

#4: CAPTURE THE FLAG
by John Vornholt

#5: ATLANTIS STATION
by V.E. Mitchell

#6: MYSTERY OF THE MISSING CREW
#7: SECRET OF THE LIZARD PEOPLE
by Michael Jan Friedman

#8: STARFALL
#9: NOVA COMMAND
by Brad and Barbara Strickland

#10: LOYALTIES
by Patricia Barnes-Svarney

#11: CROSSFIRE
by John Vornholt

#12: BREAKAWAY
by Bobbi JG Weiss and David Cody Weiss

TM, ® & © 1997 Paramount Pictures. All Rights Reserved.
Published by Pocket Books